GIVE UP
the
GHOST

GIVE UP
the
GHOST

MEGAN CREWE

HENRY HOLT AND COMPANY
New York

Henry Holt and Company, LLC
Publishers since 1866
175 Fifth Avenue
New York, New York 10010
www.HenryHoltKids.com

Library of Congress Cataloging-in-Publication Data
Crewe, Megan.
Give up the ghost / Megan Crewe.—1st ed.
p.   cm.
Summary: Sixteen-year-old Cass's only friends are her dead sister and
the school ghosts who feed her gossip that she uses to make students
face up to their bad behavior, until a popular boy asks for her help
and leads her to reach out to the living again.
ISBN 978-0-8050-8930-1
[1. Interpersonal relations—Fiction. 2. Ghosts—Fiction. 3. High
schools—Fiction. 4. Schools—Fiction. 5. Sisters—Fiction.
6. Grief—Fiction. 7. Family problems—Fiction.] I. Title.
PZ7.C86818Giv 2009   [Fic]—dc22   2008050274

First Edition—2009 / Designed by April Ward
Printed in the United States of America.
1   3   5   7   9   10   8   6   4   2

For Mom and Dad, who gave me a love for
stories before I could write a single word

GIVE UP
the
GHOST

CHAPTER 1

You would think it'd be easy to get along with a person after she's dead. Not Paige. She took her big sister duties very seriously. It'd been four years since she drowned, and she still got on my case.

"You're not really wearing *those* to school," she said, perched in the air just above the wrought-iron headboard of my bed, her ankles crossed and tipped to the side. It was the way she used to sit at the dinner table, way back when—pretending to be hooked on Dad's every word while her mind wandered off to choicer topics. Except these days she did it without a chair.

"What's wrong with them?" I asked, zipping up my jeans. She was wearing jeans, too. Of course, her jeans were tight, low-cut capris. Mine were big and baggy. I'd stepped on the hems so many times they were as thready as my violet carpet, but hey, they were comfortable.

Paige wrinkled her pert nose and shook her head. Very few things got her as worked up as my untapped fashion potential. Most of the time she had this faded tissue-paper look, so filmy I could see right through her. Get her interested, though, and she brightened up like a

Chinese lantern. Right then, she was beaming from her bleached-blond hair to her strappy sandals.

A few years ago, it would have pissed me off. These days, I was used to it. It was like a game: how bossy could she get, how bratty could I get. Playing at being normal.

"Don't you ever look at yourself, Cassie?" Paige said. "You've got nicer stuff in your closet. It's like you want to be a slob."

"There are more important things than clothes, you know."

"You could at least brush your hair. Please."

I stuck out my lip to blow my bangs away from my eyes, and grinned. "All right, if it's so important to you."

I found my brush in the heap of comic books, dirty dishes, and loose change on top of my dresser and tugged it through the mud-brown mess of my hair. Paige drifted over, her hand grazing my head with a faint tingle. The smell of candied apples and cinnamon wisped from her fingers.

"You could be pretty, Cassie," she murmured. "You've got an okay figure, if you dressed to show it off. . . . A little makeup—I bet your eyes could look really green if you did it right—and a new haircut. . . ."

"Why bother?"

Paige groaned. "You want to have friends, don't you? People care about that stuff. You look nice, they're nice to you. You look like a mess, they're laughing about it behind your back."

My smile died. I yanked the brush through a knot, wincing. From what I'd seen, looking nice didn't stop people from making fun of you. I'd dressed pretty decent back in junior high, and it sure as hell hadn't helped me.

But that was ancient history. The kids at Frazer Collegiate weren't laughing at me now. And I had enough dirt on all of them to make sure it stayed that way.

Not that I could tell that to Paige. If she knew what went on at school, she'd be ten times more freaked out than she was about my jeans.

"Do you laugh behind my back?" I asked instead.

Paige gave me her best big-sister look: eyebrows arched and lips pursed. Considering she was the same sweet-sixteen as when she'd died and I'd be seventeen in a few months, it was getting harder to take that look seriously.

"Of course not," she said. "You're my sister. I have to look out for you."

"Gee, thanks. Anyway, no one's making fun of me."

"But—"

I arched my eyebrows right back at her. "Trust me, they're not."

"Okay, okay." Her lower lip curled into a pout. "I'm just concerned. You should look after yourself. You used to . . . I think you used to make yourself up, get dressed up. Didn't you?"

I looked away. Paige hardly ever talked about things that far back. But she was right—if this had been at the beginning of seventh grade, I'd have been trying on half a dozen outfits, dabbing lipstick light enough that Mom wouldn't notice it, getting ready for another day of giggling with my friends and blushing around the boys.

A lot had changed since then. A lot that Paige hadn't wanted to see when she was alive, and now would probably never understand.

"I'm surviving just fine like this," I said, pulling my hair into an elastic. "Can we talk about something else? Besides, you should be glad. I could have a billion friends and go out every night, and then you'd be bored out of your mind."

Paige hovered over me as I stuffed last night's homework into my backpack. She didn't say anything, just watched me with her eyes all worried and her forehead crinkled. It was making me feel twisted up inside. Even after four years, it seemed weird sometimes that she paid so much attention to me.

Right before she died, Paige and I had a pretty defective relationship. Mostly it consisted of me trying to stick myself in her way and Paige doing her best to avoid me. She'd turned into a teen princess in high school, and I was a gawky tween who cramped her style. I didn't get why she didn't want me hanging out with her anymore. She didn't get why I couldn't leave her alone.

I guess I was lucky it hadn't stayed that way. Death had left Paige's fashion sense intact, but it screwed majorly with her memory. Here and there, time got stuck. Some things she talked about as if four years ago were yesterday. When Dad turned her old bedroom into a workshop, it took a month before the change worked its way into her head. Until then, she'd come bolting into my room once or twice a day, wailing about how someone had stolen all her stuff. I'd tell her what was up, she'd calm down, and then eight hours later she'd have forgotten and would freak out all over again.

But eventually Paige caught on to the things that stayed different, like the room, and like me getting older, and the now wrote over the then. In her mind, now, we've been best buds forever. And really, despite her nagging, I'd had friends a lot worse than her. At least she said what she was thinking instead of hiding it under smiles and sweet talk. The dead, maybe because they have nothing to lose, are always honest.

I put my hand on the radio. "What station do you want?"

"I don't know." Paige stared out the window gloomily, her glow dimming. "How about the hip-hop one?"

"Sure." I turned the dial and set the volume low enough that Dad wouldn't notice I'd left it on. Paige didn't move. When I looked up, she was so washed out I could see through her to the cracked paint on the window frame.

"I'll be back soon," I reminded her. "Dad should be around. And Mom . . ." I realized I didn't know where Mom was. A lump like a cherry pit stuck in my throat. Well, that was the way it went with Mom, these days. But Paige wouldn't really brighten until she came back.

"I know," Paige said, and smiled. "Thank you."

The hall floor creaked. We both went quiet. Then came Dad's trademark knock on the door: one, two, one-two-three.

"Yeah?" I said. Paige started to drift away. Dad and

Mom couldn't see or hear her. She still hung out with them sometimes—mostly with Mom, in those brief stints at home between magazine assignments—but it seemed to make her uncomfortable.

Dad eased open the door. "Hello, there," he said, studying me through the oval panes of his glasses. He rubbed the thin spot he was getting on the top of his head with his smudged fingers.

"Started the inking?" I asked. Dad took on a lot of different projects, but his favorite illustrations to do were the plain black ink ones. The last few days, he'd been working on a commissioned study of the Church of Saint Michael, so wrapped up in it he came out only for meals and our usual after-dinner TV time, when we indulged in our shared weakness for old sitcoms.

He nodded. "The mosaic tiles are quite the challenge."

"You'll have to show me as soon as it's done."

"Of course," he said, and then, "You're looking nice."

I ducked my head. "Thanks."

The funny thing was, Dad meant it. I think I could have had a wasp's nest in my hair and he'd still have thought I was lovely. For an artist, he had a strange conception of beauty.

"I thought . . . ," he began, and cleared his throat. "I need to go downtown to pick up some supplies. Would you like a ride to school?"

I glanced out the window. It was raining, a slow, steady drizzle. On the other hand, the throat-clearing suggested he was working up to an awkward conversation.

I hesitated, and instantly felt like a jerk. Dad was the last person who deserved to be snubbed.

"Sure," I said. "That would be great. When are you leaving?"

"Right now, I was hoping," he said. "But I can wait if it's too early."

"Nah, it's fine. Just let me get my stuff."

I grabbed my pack and hurried down to the front hall. Dad put on his fedora as I laced up my hiking boots. He jingled his keys against his palm with the same tune he used to knock: jing, jing, jing-jing-jing.

"So, your mother will be home for the weekend," he said. "We'll see a bit of her. I think she has another assignment starting Monday."

I shrugged. "Whatever." As if two days of playing happy homemaker could make up for the ten days she was gone. She hardly lived with us anymore.

Dad was silent as we walked out to the car, but it was the loud kind of silence that's full of things about to be said. Rain dripped off my bangs, and the T-shirt started to stick to my skin. I thought about walking. Then I thought about sitting through four classes in clammy clothes. Dad pushed open the passenger-side door from inside, and I got in.

"She misses you, you know," he said as he put his foot to the gas. The old Ford crept out of the driveway. "She wishes she could be home more."

Sure she did. Mom freelanced. She got to decide which assignments she took and which she didn't. After Paige died, she'd started writing more and more for this travel magazine, which just happened to require that she race off every second week. If she wanted to be home more, she couldn't have been doing less to make it happen.

"It's hard for her to work at home, always being in the house," Dad went on when I stayed quiet. "It reminds her. . . . She thinks a lot about your sister. It helps her to have some time away."

"No big deal," I said. "I'm used to it. Anyway, you're always here."

The buildings slid past the windows as we rolled toward Frazer. Dad hit the brakes at a red light, and we jerked to a halt. He looked over at me. The sides of his mouth were straining to keep from frowning.

"I'm sorry," he said, as if it was his fault and not hers. "She's already trying to get more local assignments. By the summer I think you'll be seeing her a lot more."

I'd been hearing that story for a couple of years now. Something always came up, some exciting lead she just had to chase, and off she'd go again. That was Mom.

"Sure," I said. Frazer loomed into sight, squatting on the school lawn like a giant quarterback. The rectangular shoulders of the east and west wings hunched behind the helmet-round head of the auditorium above and cafeteria below.

I had my hand on the door before we reached the front walk. The car lurched over a pothole and stopped. I leapt out onto the pavement, dragging my pack behind me.

"Thanks for the ride! Good luck with the inking."

I pushed the door shut before he could answer. He waved at me through the window and drove on.

The morning janitor was out on the lawn, poking at chip bags and pop cans. I hurried past him to the front door and headed up the stairs.

Like always, there were too many breathers in the halls, jostling and snickering and getting kissy-kissy in the corners. They stuck together in clumps, clogging traffic. I couldn't get two steps without some guy's elbow bumping my ribs or some girl's strawberry-kiwi—shampooed hair in my face. The humidity only made it worse.

Under it all, I caught a whiff of something only I could smell: old-fashioned hair oil. It got stronger as the crowd thinned by the hall's dead end, just past the math office, where my locker was. I smiled.

Over the years, Norris must have spent a lot of time perfecting his slouch. He leaned against the lockers, on the verge of but not quite sinking in. You could almost believe he was a real, live fourteen-year-old, held up by the wall. He raised his translucent hand to me as I squeezed past the last pod of giggling freshmen, then straightened up, lifting a few inches above the floor. He liked to imagine he was taller than me.

"Hey, Cass, how ya doing?" he said in a voice that would have been more suave if it hadn't cracked every few words. He slicked a hand over his black hair and tugged the collar of his army jacket forward. Norris didn't talk dates much, but I'd seen enough old movies to peg him as a seventies dude the moment I'd met him. He preferred the term "rebel."

"I'd be better if I didn't have to be here," I said. I spun the dial on the lock and jerked open the locker door, so it hid the movement of my mouth from the rest of the hall. "You?"

"Same old. But, hey." Norris smirked. "The kids have been busy. Wait'll you hear what I've got today."

CHAPTER 2

It made sense that the dead ended up knowing an awful lot about everyone. They spent most of their time hanging around and watching people—because, really, what else did they have to do? They were invisible and inaudible to everyone living. The things people did only when they thought they were alone, the secrets whispered between friends, all the dirt no one wanted dug up: the dead saw it and heard it. And if they found a breather with open ears, they were more than happy to tell all they knew.

For a long time, I didn't even try to listen. The first few times I'd reacted to ghosts in the halls had gotten me labeled "crazy girl" on top of everything else. Then, one day, it was like something I'd been holding tight inside slipped from my fingers and smashed. Mom had just taken off on an eight-day cruise. I'd walked down the hall to the usual stares and snickers, all too aware of how my locker neighbor mumbled some excuse and hurried off when I said hello to her. The kids who'd followed me to Frazer from junior high had done their job well. Everyone here knew I was the psycho, the boy-stealer, the greedy friend, and whatever other rumors had sprung up since. Not that they'd bothered to find out if any of it was true.

Norris and Bitzy were hanging out in the dead end by my locker. They'd been doing that a lot since they'd figured out a few months ago that I could see them. I ignored them as I grabbed the stuff I needed for that morning's classes, but I couldn't help hearing them.

"It makes me so mad!" Bitzy was saying, stamping her foot. "They pretend like they're still friends to Mary's face, but it's such an act now, and she doesn't even see it. Who does she think told that guy that she likes him so he could make fun of her? Who does she think threw her underwear in the garbage?"

My gut twisted. I shoved the book in my hand into my bag and crouched there, listening.

"How did they get her underwear?" Norris asked, focusing, of course, on the most important aspect of the situation.

"It was during swim class."

"Maybe I should run a little surveillance in the locker room—"

"Oh, gross!" Bitzy snapped. "I don't know why I even talk to you."

"Okay, I get it—it sucks. Do you have a point other than that?"

Bitzy sighed. "I just wish I could say something to her. How come it doesn't work like in the movies? I can't write on mirrors no matter how steamed up they are."

"Just let it go. People are jerks. That's life."

People are jerks. All through junior high: the giggles, the murmurs, the taunts scrawled on my locker, the shoves in the hallway. The phone left ringing in case it was yet another crank call. The textbooks held clutched on my lap so no one could bump them off my desk. Just because my supposed best friend had decided I didn't deserve her friendship or anyone else's, and everyone had gone along with what she said, glad it wasn't them being targeted. That's life.

Could anything possibly be worse than staying the way I was, the school doormat all over again?

I stood up, and I looked at Bitzy and Norris. The voice that came out of my mouth hardly sounded like my own. "I'll say something. Just tell me who it is."

Things have been a lot different since then.

Whatever Norris had this time, it had to be big. He was slouching with his thumbs slung in the belt loops of his jeans, trying to be nonchalant, but he was glowing like a lamp.

"So tell me already," I said. I leaned into my locker, shifting binders and papers in search of my geography book.

"Right." Norris leaned back against the wall and cocked his head. "You know that freshman class on the other side of the math office? There's that group of girls— Brenda and Carady and them—always yakking so loud you can hear them halfway across the school? Kind of cute, though, especially that one, Doreen." By spring, Norris had picked up all the new kids' names, even though there were three hundred of them. He remembered the cute ones particularly well.

I rummaged through my mental files. Brenda and Carady and Doreen. Yes. Playing with the hems of their skirts around Mr. Travers as if a glimpse of thigh might earn them bonus marks on their next math test. Not that they did much of their work themselves. When it came time to throw together their weekly assignments, they sucked up to a geeky girl named Lisa until she let them copy. I bet they didn't yak too loudly about that when Mr. Travers was around. ·

Norris was gazing off into space, no doubt lost in thoughts of dimpled cheeks and curvy hips. "Right," I said, calling his attention back. "What've they done now? Ragged on Lisa again?" As soon as they'd gotten what they needed from their school-smart but otherwise clueless dupe, the girls found it very entertaining to imitate her pigeon-toed walk and throaty voice to anyone within laughing distance. Real gracious to the person who kept their grades up.

"Worse. They were—" Norris frowned. He stared at the floor, scuffing his foot against the linoleum like he was trying to kick-start his memory. For new stuff, he had his shaky moments, but he did better than Paige. He could hold on to things for a few days sometimes. From what I'd seen, the longer a person's been dead, the better they remember their afterlife. Don't ask me why. Maybe practice makes perfect.

"Yesterday afternoon," he said, slowly, "yeah, in the computer lab, I just wandered in 'cause I heard them giggling, and they were all around this one computer, whispering and stuff, looking over their shoulders like they were afraid someone would catch them. Mrs. Richmond wasn't there. So I went on over to see what they were doing. They had one of those pages up, you know, where people put up pictures of themselves and talk about things they like and write comments to their friends—"

"Like a blog?" I supplied.

Norris shrugged. "Sure. Anyway, I guess this one belonged to that girl Lisa. There were a bunch of drawings up, kind of cool, really, and poems, and that kind of thing. And Brenda was writing comments about them. Really awful stuff. Saying dog piss looked prettier and she was a complete moron if she thought she could be an artist, making new poems using some of the same words but throwing in swearing and dirty stuff. . . . And they were laughing the whole time. Then Mrs. Richmond came back, and they shut it down real fast."

A chill washed over me. My thoughts flickered back to the comments I'd seen on my own computer screen, years ago: "What a backstabber! How did you manage it—made up some story, or maybe stayed after class . . . ?" "Ugh, and then going after your friend's guy. Could you get any more pathetic?" All anonymous, of course. But I'd known who'd set them talking.

"Sounds like it's worth looking into," I said, keeping my voice steady. Lisa wouldn't have a clue who'd done it, any more than she knew about the teasing that went on when she wasn't around. And she worried about enough things without getting harassed by her so-called friends. Norris had once spotted her sobbing at her desk, clutching a test on which she'd gotten just a few points short of a perfect 100 percent. "I'll see what I can do."

"I've got another one," Norris said. "Caught some more loonies trying to protect themselves from your psychic powers."

"Oh, yeah? What were they up to this time?"

"Magnets," he said. "Supposed to mess with your mental energy, or whatever. I figure they're just mental. The bunch of them, Theodore and Sandy and them, were trying to glue these little magnetic squares into their hats. And then the vice principal came along and reminded them they're not supposed to wear hats inside. So there goes that brilliant plan."

I laughed. "Hey, at least they're stretching their brains a little. Anything new with the tech squad?" A bunch of seniors had decided I had to be using wires, and spent all year searching the classrooms for bugs. So far all they'd found were centipedes.

"Nah, haven't seen them in a while. Maybe they've finally realized the beauty of what you do. I mean, really, you're doing the school a service, and the entertainment value—it's sweet all the way through."

"Hey, it's as much you as me."

Norris shook his head. "You're the general, Cass. I am honored to be your lowly lieutenant."

"That reminds me," I said. "There's some seventies war movie showing at the discount theater on Saturday. You want to go?" War movies weren't really my thing, but it was worth the ticket price to see how wrapped up Norris got, and to hear the excitement in his voice afterward.

"That'd be cool," Norris said, casually, but I saw a glint in his eyes. Then his gaze drifted. "Look, here comes the giggle gang now."

"Hurrah." I turned to watch.

Brenda, Carady, Doreen, and a couple of other girls who hung out with them were sashaying down the hall, passing a tube of lip gloss from hand to hand. Mouths shined to maximum glare, they congregated in a semicircle in front of their lockers. The way giggles erupted through the group, you'd have thought making it to school was an act of high comedy. I propped myself up against the wall on the other side of the math office door and made like I was fascinated by my geography book.

As their amusement subsided, they fell into a deep debate over which of the actors in their favorite TV show was the sexiest. I peeked at them over the top of the book, and a sharp pang hit me in the chest. We'd have looked that way, in junior high: me and Danielle and the others, standing around our lockers, gossiping about some movie star breakup or new dress style. Laughing and leaning together, voices squealing.

My throat choked up with longing, and my eyes felt like they were about to overflow. I blinked quickly, gritting my teeth and shoving the memories away.

God, I had been so stupid. To think we were talking about important things. To think the fact that we were talking like that, together, meant anything at all.

And here I was, still missing the way things had been. Even stupider.

A few words slipped out of the chatter and snapped me back to reality.

"Can you believe . . . that assignment—"

"I know, it's so insane."

I edged a little closer. Assignment time meant playing friends with Lisa time. Could they really smile to her face after ripping her up like that yesterday?

It looked like I was about to find out. A tall girl in a long, loose skirt was shuffling down the hall toward the row of lockers. Her shirt was buttoned wrong and her bangs stuck up in several different directions. I caught myself wondering if she owned a mirror, then remembered my conversation with Paige that morning. Maybe Lisa just had other things she thought were more important.

There was something different about her today, though. She walked slower, her shoulders slumped, and as she passed the other girls and came up to her locker, I could see puffiness around her eyes.

Then Carady called out, "Hey, Lisa!" and Lisa's face brightened so much you'd have thought she'd just been announced valedictorian. She smiled shyly, her shoulders straightening as Brenda and the others sauntered over and a knot of doubt formed inside me. Would it really help her, knowing the girls she obviously admired had been the ones attacking her? Or would it just make her even more miserable?

She deserves to know, I told myself. And they deserve to know they can't just get away with it.

The girls had gathered around Lisa, Doreen playing with Lisa's stringy hair, Carady patting her arm, Brenda going so far as to offer the sacred lip gloss. Lisa blushed as she slicked it on. They were all smiling, smiling with lots of teeth.

"So, Lisa," Brenda said, simperingly, "you wanna hang out with us after school today? Maybe we could check our assignments, and then go grab some fries or something. It'd be so much fun."

Translation: The other girls would copy down Lisa's assignment, making enough small mistakes so it wouldn't be completely obvious, and then they'd all suddenly realize they had really important things to run off and do.

But there was Lisa, beaming, her mouth already opening to say she'd love to.

I set my book down on the floor and walked up to the circle. "Funny," I said, "that's not the way you were talking yesterday."

The girls fell silent. Brenda crossed her arms over her chest, her jaw twitching. These days, my reputation had its benefits. They knew who I was. Cass McKenna, that crazy girl who knows the dirt on everyone.

"Who was talking to you?" Brenda said, rolling her eyes, but her voice wavered and her friends giggled nervously.

"I'm talking to *you*," I said. "And I think it's pretty strange that you're being so friendly with Lisa here after what happened yesterday. Or do you always expect favors from people you bash?"

Lisa's gaze darted from the girls to me and back again, her expression showing nothing more than confusion.

"I don't know what you mean," Brenda said. "We're friends. We help each other out. Right, Lisa?"

"Yeah, of course," Lisa mumbled.

I raised my eyebrows. "I guess you need your memory jogged. 'My dog's piss looks better than this.' 'You're a moron, not an artist.' Ring any bells?"

A little cry slipped from Lisa's mouth.

"You've got no proof," Brenda snapped. Suddenly all her friends were finding the floor inexplicably fascinating.

"We could take a walk down to the computer lab and see if the one you were logged in to yesterday has a certain blog in its browsing history," I offered.

Doreen broke then. "No!" she whined. "We're sorry, really, we won't do it again. Just don't tell the teachers. My mom—"

"Shut up!" Brenda said, too late. Lisa slammed her locker shut and hurried away from them, her shoulders trembling. "Lisa!" Brenda called after her.

"Leave me alone!" Lisa yelled back, and threw open the door of the bathroom to stomp inside.

Brenda spun around. "You better watch your step," she said to me.

Like it was my fault she was a lying, cheating snob. I gritted my teeth. "Maybe you should watch yours."

The anger in her face faltered. She had no idea what else I might know.

No one was willing to take that chance.

"Oh, my God!" one of the girls exclaimed as I walked away. "How are we going to get the homework done now?"

Norris was hovering back where I'd left him, grinning his face off.

I picked up my geography book. "Enjoy that?"

"Oh, yeah. Pow! Pow!" He took a couple of boxer jabs at the air. "If you weren't a girl, I'd have to say, 'You are the man.'"

"Thanks." I stared at the aluminum locker door with its splotches of dried gum and permanent marker. Would things be better now for Lisa? Or would the girls find some way to make nice and she'd fall for their act all over again? Sometimes people backed off. Sometimes it worked. But sometimes they just got smarter about their lies.

I glanced toward the washroom door. Lisa would be bawling her eyes out. Then the warning bell rang, reminding everyone they had five minutes to get to class, and I shook the uneasiness away.

"I'd better get going," I said.

"Course. You'll come by later?"

I glanced at Norris, and he dropped his gaze. "Not that it's a huge deal if you don't," he added.

"Norris," I said, "I'll hang out with you whenever you want. You're practically the only person with any sense in this entire school. What's going on? You not talking to Bitzy?"

"She's not talking to me," he said.

"No? What, did you call her fat again?" He ducked his head, and I groaned. "Norris, you know how she feels about the F-word. You want her to stop talking to you for good? It's going to happen if you can't stop crap like that from coming out of your mouth."

Norris grimaced. "She was getting on my case about the locker room. It's not all my fault."

I shook my head at him. "Well, you're going to have to start finding better ways to argue. I'll see if I can talk her down. But you've got to go apologize. And next time, you're on your own."

CHAPTER

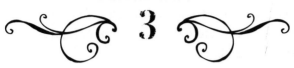

3

Because of the Lisa incident, I had to postpone my usual check-in with Bitzy until lunch. Coming down the hall toward the gym, I heard her mumbling before I saw her. "Where is she? Where is she already?" The girl was a little impatient. I scooted around a bend in the hallway, and there she was, bobbing up and down on her toes by the gym door and blazing light through her leotard.

Bitzy claimed she was a born ballerina. She couldn't stay in one spot without stretching out her legs or spinning around in a pirouette. For all that practice, she wasn't exactly the most graceful person I'd ever encountered.

"Cass!" she shrieked as I walked over. She hurtled across the hall to me. One of the gym teachers barged right through her, and she didn't even blink. I met her eyes and shot a look at the pay phone in the alcove beside the trophy case. She followed me over.

"Oh, my God, oh, my God, oh, my God!" she whispered the whole way there, punctuating it with little squeals of excitement. She lifted her arms over her head and tiptoed the last few steps, adding a wobbly twirl at the end, the scent of lemon-polished wood drifting with her.

The tip of her ponytail sparkled. Either Bitzy had stumbled onto the juiciest gossip known to mankind, or she was about to go supernova.

Still, the first thing she said when I picked up the phone was, "Norris is such a perv. You know he was hanging out in the girls' locker room again? Somebody oughta pound him."

I shifted the earpiece so the dial tone droned into my hair, and pretended I was talking to someone on the other end. "You know, Bitz, from what he's said about his dad, I think he's been pounded plenty already." Heck, the guy was dead, and staring at half-naked girls fed his hormones about as much as Bitzy's avoidance of the cafeteria shrank her waistline. "It's just a habit," I added. "He can't help it."

"Well, I don't like it," she said. "He . . . he was really nasty to me."

I grimaced. I couldn't argue with that. "Yeah, he mentioned that. But you know sometimes Norris talks more than he thinks. You guys have been sharing the school for how many years now?"

"I was here first," she said. "And I'm not going to put up with people talking mean about me anymore."

"You're right. He really shouldn't talk to you like that. I told him to cut it out. And he seems sorry."

"Yeah?" Bitzy's voice softened. "Well, I still don't feel like talking to him today."

"Hey, that's up to you." Maybe if Norris got a couple more days of the cold shoulder, he'd remember to watch his mouth next time. I relaxed back against the wall. "So what's the big news?"

Bitzy's face brightened up like I'd flicked a switch. "Oh, Cass, you're just going to die. It's got something to do with *her*."

Her? Danielle.

Bitzy kept talking, but I hardly heard her.

Just thinking of Danielle gave me the same feeling as years ago, on a trip to Florida, when a wave had dragged my feet out from under me and smacked me into the sea bottom: the current roaring past my ears, my chest aching with held breath. Memories crashed over me: tossing popcorn at each other on sleepover nights, giggling our heads off trying on bikinis in the mall, teasing each other's hair into crazy dos . . . and then my stomach sinking as my name echoed out of the PA system one late winter morning in seventh grade. Me going to the statewide debate competition—not her. Me going with the guy she'd had her eye on all year, the guy she'd joined the debate team for in the first place.

There were a few hours when, amid the congratulations and the high fives, I'd thought maybe my terror was unreasonable. She was my friend. She'd be happy for me. I'd talk her up to Cameron, and we'd all be happy. Ha ha ha.

Even the terror hadn't prepared me for how fast and how hard it came. The images were like glints of broken glass: her sneer against the bronzed shine of her hair, the notes crinkling from hand to hand around my desk, the backs turned with hers in the middle, tallest. The heel of her shoe crushing my toes in the hall; the pop bottle emptied over the contents of my locker, which only she'd had the combination to. The words scrawled in handwriting I knew almost as well as my own, on the bathroom wall for everyone to see——CASS IS A SKANK.

And that had just been the beginning.

Because a teacher had picked me over her? Because I'd accidentally grabbed a piece of her spotlight? The unfairness of it, even four years later, made my throat tighten. I coughed and sucked in air.

"Cass?" Bitzy was saying. "Hey, Cass? Dontcha want to hear it?" She hopped from side to side like she was about to pee her pants.

I breathed and swallowed, breathed again. The crashing feeling washed away. The phone had slipped down to my shoulder. A couple of girls stared at me as they flounced by, and I brought it back to my mouth. "Course," I said. "Spill it."

"Okay. So, you know she's been going with Paul for, like, forever now. Well, I was watching the boys' track practice this morning, and Paul's on the team. This girl— she had crazy highlights, and she was wearing those super-tight jeans and a baby-doll top. . . ." She paused, crinkling her forehead. "Sharry! That's what he called her. She came over to the fence to watch—she's a sophomore, I think."

"Sharon Lietzer," I murmured. How could any guy resist a girl best known for the things she could do with her tongue? Paul had been hanging around with her last year before Danielle had set her sights on him.

"Anyway," Bitzy said, "she came and waved at him, and after the coach dismissed them, Paul went over to talk to her. Acting all hip, flexing and stuff, trying to impress her. In, like, five seconds they're hiding in the equipment shed behind the bleachers, making out all over the place, and after a bit she says, 'What about Danielle?' and he laughs and says, 'I won't tell her if you don't.' And then they almost did it."

"Did it?" I said. "You mean he was going to have sex with her?"

"Well. . . ." Bitzy blushed and looked at her feet. For someone who adored this kind of gossip, she could be a bit of a prude about it. "All the clothes stayed on. So they didn't actually . . . do it. But I think they might have if the warning bell hadn't rung. They were really going at it."

"Wow." My skin felt cool and clammy, like I had been swimming in the ocean, but inside I was burning up. This was like a gift, just handed to me. A free pass to rip the sneer off Danielle's face.

I'd heard her in the halls, so loud I didn't need Norris or Bitzy to tell me about it, bragging to Jordana and the rest of her girlfriends about Paul. "He's such a gentleman, you know," she'd gush. "I mean, he never pressures me at all. Totally cool with waiting. And he's always telling me how lucky he is that he's got me."

Every now and then, someone might ask, "Didn't he used to date Sharon Lietzer?"

Danielle would smile. "He took one look at me and never looked back. She can have all the other guys she wants—I've got the sweetest one in the school."

Sure. So sweet that by tomorrow morning Sharon might have eaten him up.

A memory flashed through my mind: sixth grade, the

Christmas dance. Danielle's face red from bawling, after her crush spent the entire dance arm in arm with another girl. Back then I had comforted her.

Back then she would have comforted me.

I swallowed the lump in my throat. Poor Danielle. Looks like you don't get to have everything after all. You steal a guy from someone, why shouldn't she try to steal him back? Guess your gentleman's more interested in getting his hands in a girl's pants than waiting for that perfect moment. He duped you as easily as you duped me.

In the end, she'd done it to herself. I was just speeding up the process.

I nibbled at my chapped lips. Not that I was going to dump it all in her lap just yet. Danielle deserved some squirming time. She'd drawn my torture out for ages. Why should I go easy on her?

"What are you going to do?" Bitzy whispered.

"Right away? Just bat them around a bit." I hung up the phone. "I think I'll start now."

Bitzy squeezed herself and spun around on one foot. "Oh, I can't wait. I'm coming, too."

I'd walked the distance from the phone alcove to the cafeteria so many times I knew the steps by heart. Twenty to the corner, fifteen more to the doors. With each step, anticipation turned into exhilaration, making my feet light. My hands smudged the glass doors as I pushed inside. Bitzy lingered in the doorway.

"You coming?" I murmured. "Come on, Bitzy, you can walk through walls. Being around a little junk food isn't going to weigh you down."

She frowned. "I know," she said. "I know I can't eat it. But I still want to. And wanting to makes me feel like a tub of lard."

"Okay," I said. "But there's never going to be another one like this."

As I left her, a desperate voice called from a stand near the doors. "Prom ticket? They're fifty percent off!"

That was how much school spirit sucked at Frazer; they couldn't even sell table spots at the prom. The seniors wanted to jet down to Cancún instead. I glanced at the poor kid they had peddling tickets and, in my good mood, shot him a smile of sympathy. He looked at me blankly for a second, then became very busy studying his pile of unsold tickets. I dropped my gaze.

If he wasn't avoiding you, he'd be laughing at you, I reminded myself. Take your pick.

I weaved around the clumps of chairs, deeper into the cafeteria. The ceiling was so low a pro basketball player would have had to hunch, and it made the whole place look dark, even with the fluorescent panels overhead. At one of the side pillars, I paused, considering the best approach. A couple of girls glanced over at me, and the babble of voices at their tables hushed. As if I was listening to them. All I could hear was my heartbeat.

Dead ahead was the central pillar, ringed by a wide, legless tabletop. The center table belonged to Very Important People, a group that at any given time might include student councillors, newspaper staff, sports stars and their most devoted fans. They weren't half so important to the rest of the school as they were to themselves,

and it wasn't like anyone else wanted that table, anyway
The way it was built around the pillar, they couldn't see
half the people sitting there without straining their necks.

None of them looked up as I edged closer—too fascinated with themselves. I knew the faces of the center table
regulars so well I barely needed to touch my mental files.

1. Tim, student council vice president. Very popular
   with the girls, even more so now that he was mourning the death of his mom. Never seemed to have an
   actual girlfriend, though. Probably a player.
2. Flo, head editor for the school paper. Maintained a
   well-earned reputation for sticking her nose where it
   didn't belong. Had a thing for Leon.
3. Leon, student council secretary. Flirted with Flo con-
   stantly but had said he'd sooner date a dog.
4. Jordana, junior class rep. Backstabber of supposed
   friends. Chatted up other guys to make her boyfriend
   jealous, then got offended when he was pissed.
5. Matti, Jordana's boyfriend, head of the student ath-
   letic association and all-around creep. Nabbed by
   yours truly for selling fake exam copies back when I
   first got started. Also a backstabber.
6. Paul, Danielle's boyfriend, track star, captain of the
   basketball team, and supposed gentleman. Fondler of
   Sharon Lietzer.
7. The permed and polished Danielle Perry, all-around
   popular girl and the biggest backstabber of them all.

All present and accounted for.
My pulse was really pounding by then, but it wasn't

hard to guess what they were saying. Every lunch hour, they had the same conversation.

Flo: "The *Frazer Gazette* needs more juice. Give me some business to stick my nose into."

Leon: "Student council affairs are confidential, but because it's you, here's a tidbit and a wink."

Jordana, fluttering her eyelashes: "Uh-oh, what if I tattle on you?"

Matti: "How dare you flutter your eyelashes at someone else! Don't you know ten girls tried to take me home last night?"

Danielle: "You guys should break up already. Can't you see Paul and I are the ones in tru luv?"

Paul: "That's right, babe. Let's prove it by sucking each other's tongues off."

Tim, with his patented pained-but-brave smile: "My mom died. Doesn't brooding look good on me?"

Everyone else: "Poor Tim!"

Flo: "But I already used that story."

Danielle: "I'm bored. Where's that tongue, lover boy?"

For Danielle lunch consisted almost entirely of saliva du Paul. Must have been how she stayed so skinny. Either that, or she did her puking at home where Bitzy couldn't catch her, unlike half the other girls at Frazer. I hated to admit it, but she was smarter than most. Even with Norris and Bitzy sicced on her, the best they'd dug up until now was a little catfighting. She always seemed to clean up her trash before I stumbled on it. Even though she'd spent the entire time since we'd entered high school pretending I didn't exist, she must have noticed that not much escaped me these days.

I hung back behind the nearest table, waiting for her to stop swapping spit long enough for me to get a word in. As I watched, this shrimpy freshman girl with barrettes and bubble-gum pink lipstick crept up to the other side of the table. She had a wrapped chocolate bar clutched tight against her chest.

"Tim," she said in a wispy voice, bowing her head like she was addressing a god, "the machine gave me two bars by mistake. I thought, maybe, you might want one."

Tim forced a smile again. It didn't quite reach the edges of his lips. He always smiled the exact same way, as if he rehearsed it every night for maximum sympathy production.

I'm sure he really was torn up about his mom. Having someone die on you—no one needed to tell me how much that sucked. But no matter how sad he was, it didn't excuse his using it to work the ladies. Or keeping the company he did.

He inclined his head so his blond hair drifted over his forehead and half closed his eyes. "Thanks," he said, "really," and took the chocolate bar.

The girl bobbed on her feet and scurried away.

"Pathetic," Danielle said, flouncing her hair. The bronze highlights shimmered, and my fingers curled. I shoved my hands into my pockets so she wouldn't see them shaking, and exhaled in a slow stream. My heart was thundering in my head like a crazed bull, but my voice— my voice was steady.

"Hey, Paul," I said, stepping up to the table.

He swiveled in his chair, his eyebrows cocked, his

lips parting to make some snappy remark. Then his eyes hit mine. His expression stuttered. Panic flashed across his face.

"What?" he said as he re-created his look of casual indifference. His hand on the back of his chair was still clenched, the knuckles going white. I had him, and he knew it. And Danielle was going to know it, too.

They were all staring at me now. My mouth had gone dry. But I had to do it this way, so everyone would hear, so everyone would be whispering about her, this time.

I pushed my lips into a smile. "How's it going?"

"Fine," he said.

His hand slipped down to grasp Danielle's. She glared at me, her mouth tight. "Piss off, Cassie." So angry and scared that her voice came out scratchy.

The tables had turned. She had asked for this from the moment she'd whispered the first bad words about me around the school, from the moment she'd turned up her nose at me like I was suddenly the lowest scum on the planet, because someone had dared to give me one little thing she'd wanted.

"So," I said to Paul, dragging in a breath, "I hear you've really been enjoying track practice lately."

"I guess. What's it to you?"

He must have thought it was brave, pushing the issue. It was just stupid.

"Well . . . the field belongs to everybody. So anything that happens out there, it's as much my business as yours."

Blood rushed into Paul's face, splotching his cheeks. Danielle's pearly nails dug into his arm.

"Yeah?" he said.

I cocked my head. The trembling in my hands, the pounding of my heart, none of it mattered now.

"So be careful you haven't been enjoying the equipment shed too much. You know what I mean."

The moment was brilliantly clear. Danielle shifting, her mouth opening. Paul gaping, speechless. Frozen. Perfect.

"See you later," I said, and he blinked. The cafeteria crowd swallowed me up before any of them could say a word.

CHAPTER 4

I coasted through the day, the anticipation of victory dissolving in my mouth like a butterscotch candy. This had all started with Danielle. Maybe if she fell, deflated and disgraced, I could finally forget about her and everything she'd done.

During my last-period study hall, I stopped by my locker to see Norris before taking off. He wasn't there. My mind started replaying the shock on Danielle's face as I jiggled open the lock, which was why I didn't notice right away what fluttered out of the ventilation slats in the locker door. It wisped as it hit the floor. I glanced down. A piece of notepaper, folded, lay beside the toe of my boot. The outer fold said *Cass* in narrow, jagged handwriting.

Dread soured my mouth.

No, this wasn't junior high. These days, Cass McKenna could handle a little note. Maybe I had a secret admirer. Ha.

I picked it up and unfolded it. The scrawl got narrower.

I know how you know. Meet me at the basketball courts, final bell, this afternoon.

"What's that?"

Norris drifted out of the wall and peered over my shoulder. Before he could read it, I crumpled the note into a ball and stuffed it into my pocket.

"Just the vaguest message in the history of the universe," I said, tossing a couple books into the bottom of my locker. Someone was trying to intimidate me, obviously. Maybe Brenda wanting to get back at me for this morning?

"Oh. Well, he did look like a vague kind of guy," Norris said.

I stopped in midtoss, a binder dangling between my fingers. "You saw who put it there?"

"Sure," Norris said, taking a swipe at his hair. As if he was ever going to smooth down that ducktail now. "It was that Tim guy. You know him—tall, thin, kind of gloomy looking. One of the student council guys."

"Yeah, I know him," I said, staring up at Norris. "What the hell happened?"

"Well, first he comes wandering over here, all casual, right around the end of lunch." Norris strutted down the hall in imitation. "When the bell rings and everybody scrams, he seems to think it's safe to slip the thing in your locker. Little did he know," Norris concluded, jerking up his jacket collar, "nothing escapes the great and powerful Norris."

Nothing except a sane reason for Tim Reed to be sticking notes in my locker. The ladies' man VP secretly corresponding with the terror of Frazer Collegiate? Any second, the ceiling was going to crash down on our heads. I threw the binder into my locker, frowning.

"He's the one whose mom died, right?" Norris said.

"Yeah," I replied. "That's him." There had been such a fuss over it that even Norris remembered. The male teachers patting Tim on the back and offering him extensions on his assignments; the female teachers enveloping him in awkward hugs. Every girl, freshman through senior, throwing him glossy-eyed looks of sympathy and a chance at their virginity (or lack thereof). I was sorry that anyone ever had to lose their mom, him included. But, really, who needed their grief made public in a weeklong school fund-raiser/mournfest, complete with cheerleaders shouting "Noooo to cancer!"?

It didn't help that the whole time I couldn't stop thinking about Paige. How, when she'd died, it'd been all over the news, so everyone at Washington Junior High should have known I'd lost my sister. And not one of my classmates had said a word.

"I don't get it. He's got the whole school wrapped around his finger. Why's he bugging me?"

"Maybe he did something and he's trying to get to you before you out him," Norris suggested.

"You see anything?"

"Nope. Whatever he does with all those girls who chase him, he doesn't do it here."

I ran through my mental files. Bitzy had seen Tim dent another guy's car in the school parking lot a while back, but he'd played the good guy and written a check.

Then it hit me. "Of course."

"What?" Norris said. "You got something on him?"

"Not exactly," I said. "He's friends with a guy I had a little chat with this morning. Probably thinks he can talk me out of telling the whole thing." Maybe he figured all he'd have to do was make his pained smile at me and say a few solemn words, and I'd fall over to please him like every other girl.

Not likely. I had front-row seats to watching Danielle find out what it was like to be betrayed, and I wasn't giving them up for anything.

"Thanks for keeping an eye on things, Norris," I said, closing the locker door.

"Not a problem. I do what I can."

"You know, there's something else you could do, if you don't mind."

"Hey, anything," he said, sinking lower.

"I've told you to keep an eye on Danielle before, right? And her boyfriend?"

"Yeah, I remember. Danielle and Paul. And those other losers, their friends—"

"Don't worry about the friends right now," I said, looking him straight in the eyes so he'd know how important this was. "Can you keep an extra-close eye on Paul, especially around track practice?"

Norris hesitated. "Bitzy likes to hang out around the field in the morning."

"Yeah, well, maybe you'll have to grovel a little. I think she'd appreciate it." I raised my eyebrows at him. "Don't be one of the jerks. This is really important, and two sets of eyes are better than one."

"Okay, okay. I'll handle it."

"Thanks. I'm going to jet—we'll talk more tomorrow, all right? And we're on for Saturday?"

"Definitely," Norris said, giving me a thumbs-up. I tipped my head to him and headed down the hall. Sorry, Tim, but I'm not available for any pleading sessions for Paul at present. Let him make his own case, if he cares.

Outside, I dragged in a breath. I didn't feel like sticking around to see what Tim had to say, but I wasn't in much of a mood to go home to Paige's makeup tips or Dad's wordless concern either. For a little while, it'd be nice to have a place where there was no one but me.

The breeze lifted over me, carrying the scent of the lake all the way up from the bay. Without thinking, I followed it.

As I meandered south, my gaze slid over the windows of the houses I passed. In one or two on every street, I caught glimpses of faces that weren't quite right. They would lean right through the glass, or hover with the sunlight passing through them instead of hitting the skin. A translucent little girl waved at me from a balcony, but I pretended I couldn't see. She didn't expect me to. After that, I kept my eyes on the pavement.

Finally, I reached the busy four-lane road that separated the residential neighborhoods from the park by the bay. The cars roared by while I waited for the light to change. A couple of vehicles that looked more like cardboard boxes than cars sagged on their wheels in the beach's barren parking lot, waiting for owners who were probably visiting the nearby seniors' center. It was too early for after-work joggers and too late for nannies to bring their screaming charges to the playground. The perfect time. I followed the parallel green and blue lines in the middle of the bicycle path down to the playground, where I crunched across the pebbles to the swing set and flopped down on the only untangled swing.

A long time ago, this had been Paige's favorite place. She'd come down to the beach all the time, with her friends, with her boyfriend, Larry, showing off her newest swimsuit or charging around on her roller skates. Always ended up jumping in the water. Before she'd decided I was the most annoying kid on the planet, she used to let me tag along.

I swayed from side to side, bumping against the other swings. The lake was behind me, out of sight, but I could hear it. The waves rose and fell against the sand like the breath of a person sleeping. Off to the east where the beach got chunky with rocks, there was a battered plywood fence that leaned over so far in spots it touched the ground. Just beyond the fence stood the old fishing hut, and its dock, snaking twenty, maybe thirty, feet into the water.

No one fished in the lake anymore—most of the fish had succumbed to acid rain—but that didn't stop the hut from stinking like a seafood restaurant's Dumpster. You had to go out on the dock to get away from it. Out to where the boards sagged and creaked with patches of rot and needly splinters.

Right near the end of the dock, there was a nail where she'd have hooked her clothes before diving in. She hadn't known that the wind would whip up, snatch her dress, and toss it out onto the waves. There'd been six of them there, and not one had thought that the start of a thunder-shower might be a bad time to go skinny-dipping.

I closed my eyes, but the sound of the waves just got

louder. It'd been stupid to come here. Sure, I was alone. The ghosts raised by the lake were only in my head—the one place I couldn't walk away from.

After a while, the breeze started to cool off, tickling goose bumps on my arms. Laughter drifted into the playground. I opened my eyes as a bunch of elementary school kids raced across the pebbles, claiming the remaining swings. Must have come from the public school down the street. I'd been sitting there my whole spare hour. Final bell would have already rung at Frazer.

Enough moping around. If I didn't head home soon, Paige would start fretting about how late I was.

As I ambled along the bike path, shoes scraped the grass behind me. The footsteps matched my pace. The parking lot came into view, and I walked a little faster. The person behind me sped up, too. Great. Some joker was trying to creep me out. Gritting my teeth, I turned around to tell him off. I almost tripped over my feet.

Coming to a stop on a patch of turf, his bony hands stuffed into the pockets of his khakis and his eyes fixed on me, was Mr. VP himself.

The last time I'd been followed was in eighth grade, by a bunch of guys who thought it'd be funny to throw rocks at my legs and see if I could dodge them. Other girls, maybe, would have been flattered by Tim's determination. But this was me, and all I felt was freaked out.

"What are you doing here?" I said. "Are you stalking me or something?"

"What? No. I— It's—" Tim cleared his throat and shrugged his shoulders back, seeming even taller as he did it. The sun behind him bleached his hair white. He stepped toward me.

"Look, I was skipping history," he said, "and I saw you leaving. That note—you got the note, right? I wanted to talk to you, and it looked like you weren't going to stick around. So I followed you."

Clearly our definitions of stalking differed.

I glared at him. "And then you hung around watching me? Real cool."

"You, like, kind of . . . ," he started, then revised. "It didn't seem like you'd want anyone bothering you. So I waited."

"Well, guess what? I still don't want anyone bothering me."

It would have been a grand dramatic exit, me storming off with my chin high, if Tim hadn't shifted in front of me and blocked my way, his arms outstretched.

"I'd like to leave now," I said, trying to maneuver around him. He moved with me.

"Just wait, one minute, please." He half closed his eyes the way he had when the girl had given him the chocolate bar: heavy-lidded with pain.

"You can't say anything that'll stop me from ratting out Paul," I said, "so you might as well save it."

He blinked. His eyebrows drew together, then broke apart as he laughed. "You think I'm here because of that idiot? You can bash Paul all you want. It sounds like he has it coming."

"Oh." I shifted my balance from one foot to the other, eyeing him. "So what do you want, then?"

The laugh had left him grinning—for real, not the usual pained expression. I could see how he could have charmed a thousand girls, smiling like that. It suggested that we were in on it together, some joke on Paul. For a second, I half believed he wanted to help me put an end to that guy's crap. Curiosity held me there, waiting to hear what he would say.

"You know stuff," he said. "You find out everything that happens at Frazer, and no one knows how."

"Yeah?" I said.

"Well, how do you do it?"

"I thought you already knew," I said. "Isn't that what your note said?"

"Well, some people say maybe you're psychic, or it's some weird magic, like witchcraft. There's got to be something."

This time, I laughed. "You think I'm a witch?"

"I don't know," he said, a hint of frustration creeping into his voice. His smile disappeared. "That's why I'm asking you." He moved forward, and I stepped backward, shifting so I had a clear path toward the parking lot.

"So you lied?" I said. "That *really* makes me want to talk to you."

"I didn't think you'd listen to me if I didn't say something that would get your attention. . . . I guess you're not really listening anyway. I'm sorry, okay? I just—you obviously can do *something* no one else can, and I thought, it seemed like . . . I just want to know what you do."

"And why did you think I was going to tell you? That's the part I'm not getting."

"I—I need to know," he said, lamely.

"Okay," I said. "Whatever. You want to tell me what for, at least?"

"What?"

"What do you want to know for?" I asked. "Why's it such a big deal that you went to all this trouble?"

He sighed. "It's just—it's important."

"Oh, come on," I said. "You don't usually expect people you've never talked to to spill their guts just like that, do you? Why do you want to know?"

"I told you, it's important. Can't you just believe me?"

"Hey, you're the one who followed me all the way down here. If you can't be bothered to tell me—"

He stepped forward again, giving me an excuse to move closer to the parking lot. "You're making this really hard, you know."

And that was the end of my patience. This was, of course, all about him. He had the right to follow me, to watch me, to demand answers, but I didn't have the right to ask the most obvious question. Who the hell did he think he was?

"Why should I make it easy?" I asked, edging farther away. "You haven't given me any reason to say anything to you. I hardly know you. We've never even talked before."

Tim stared at me. Apparently he thought his asking should be reason enough.

"Fine," he said, his voice shaking. "If you want to make it hard, I can handle hard. You want to swear me to secrecy? I'll swear on my mom's grave. Will that make you happy?"

The strap of his shoulder bag slipped down his arm, and I gained a car length as he yanked it back onto his shoulder. My feet slipped off the grass and onto the parking lot pavement. He strode after me, his face tight.

I couldn't believe him. Angry at me, as if I was somehow harassing him. And bringing his mom into it for a pity play—was he trying to win an award for jerkdom, or what?

"Hey," I said. "I don't owe it to you to tell you. I don't owe you anything. So there's one person in the world who doesn't jump when you snap your fingers. Deal with it."

Then I turned and walked away.

I tried to make that last little speech brutal enough to stop him cold. But I was only halfway across the parking lot when his sneakers hit the asphalt behind me, hurrying to catch up. The air shifted as he reached toward me.

"Okay, look, if you'd wait a second—"

My hands clenched in frustration. He wasn't going to leave me alone. Instinct yanked me forward. I didn't want to listen anymore. I just wanted to get away. Head down, I sprinted toward the traffic lights.

The lights were changing to red as I scrambled over the median and jogged toward the elementary school. A horn blared, and I realized Tim had raced through the red light after me. What would it take for this guy to give up? I did the only thing I could think of: I ran faster.

"Cass," he shouted, "will you stop? This is stupid. I'm just—" He lost the rest of his sentence in a gasp of air. I dodged a sidewalk shelf of produce, skidding on the pulp of a fallen tomato. As I barreled toward the curb, a woman pushed her stroller around the corner and smack into my way. I stumbled to the side, arms flailing to catch my balance, and Tim snatched at my shoulder. The base of the stroller crashed into his knee. The baby started wailing like the world was ending, and Tim toppled over like a tree, his bag flying. He caught himself before his knees hit the sidewalk and crouched there, panting. The bag thudded onto the cement a few feet away. A couple of books spilled out.

I glanced down at them, lying faceup on the sidewalk, and froze.

One was *Thirteen Conversations with the Dead.* The other, *The Idiot's Guide to the Afterlife.* Spooky clouds decorated the covers, shot through with beams of moonlight, here a crystal ball, there a crooked tree. My stomach twisted.

"I'm so sorry," Tim was saying to the stroller lady. His voice echoed, the way outside sounds do when you're miles away inside your head. All I saw was the books. Swallowing the acid taste in my mouth, I knelt down to pick one up.

The table of contents read like a cheesy TV exposé: "Dealing with the Dead," "The Mystery of the Medium," "Signs of the Spirits." The illustration showed a gypsy woman sitting at a table with a bowl of water, ghostly figures swirling in the air above her like smoke from a pie she'd left in the oven too long. Any other time I'd have laughed and tossed the book away. That woman and I had zilch in common. But the guy who'd been carrying it had just chased me across two blocks like a maniac.

He couldn't know. It was impossible . . . wasn't it?

I stood up, gingerly. Tim was hunched over, helping

the stroller lady fix a wheel that had gotten stuck off-kilter. She popped it into place, glared at me like it was my fault some guy had decided to terrorize me, and rolled the screaming baby away. Tim reached for his bag, shoving the other book into it. I watched and waited, my teeth clenched so tightly my jaw started to ache. He turned, looked at me, and saw the book in my hand.

"You think you're so smart, don't you?" I snapped. "Pretending you don't know anything, acting all clueless. What're these about, then?"

His mouth tensed. "Give me that. I was just . . . It's none of your business."

"None of my business? Excuse me, aren't you the one who just chased me down?"

He was staring at me as if he had no clue what I meant. Crap. Maybe he didn't know. And I'd almost—

"Never mind," I said. "Forget it. I'm getting out of here."

I threw the book down, whipped around, and stomped off toward home.

This time, he let me go, only his gaze trailing after me. I could feel it on my back. In a way, it was worse than if he'd charged after me again. I didn't know what he was thinking, but I could tell that whatever it was, it meant only trouble.

CHAPTER 5

Paige barged through my bedroom door the next morning as I was getting dressed. "Maybe looks are the wrong thing to focus on. I think you need to get a hobby," she announced. "Or find a cool place to hang out."

I didn't like the sound of this. "What for?"

"If you're doing something interesting, people'll want to get to know you. Maybe you'd be happier."

"Who says I'm not happy?"

Paige rolled her eyes. "Please. I'm your sister, I can tell. When was the last time you had friends over or went out to a party?"

"Maybe I prefer the company I already have," I said. The kind that talked to me regardless of what I was wearing or what anyone said about me. The kind I could count on not to have a sudden change of heart and ditch me.

"Sure," Paige said, sighing. "Anyway, first you should—"

Before she could continue, I burrowed into the closet where I could pretend to be deaf. In the dusty dark, squished between a sweater and a pair of corduroys, my breath was even louder than her voice. Everything in there smelled like the fabric softener Mom had used since I was a baby, soft and powdery. When I was little, she washed my sheets every week and my whole bed smelled like that. It was the smell of sick days, lying in bed with Mom hovering over me, blowing cool air like a ghost's kiss on my fevered forehead. If I stayed in there long enough, the hot press of the clothes made me feel like I really did have a fever.

This time, remembering those moments with Mom made me think of Tim. Or rather, Tim's dead mom.

That whole thing yesterday had to be because of her, of course. That was what the books were for. But he'd also been so persistent about talking to me. Just how much did he know? And how did he know anything at all?

The side of my face tingled as Paige seeped through the clothes and leaned close to me. "Are you okay, Cassie?" she asked.

I hauled myself out of the closet with a burgundy hoodie and black cargoes. "I'm fine," I said.

Was it possible Tim had seen his mom the way I'd seen Paige that first time? What if that was why he wanted to talk to me? But those questions just led me back to the first—how had he known to pick on me? If I'd screwed up badly enough that he'd figured something out, did other people know, too?

Paige was scowling at my choice of clothing.

"You always wear stuff that's so dark," she said. "It's depressing. How about a little color for once?"

"Yeah, yeah," I said, wobbling as I stepped into the pants, "and don't forget to wash behind my ears and floss after breakfast. I already have a mom, thanks."

Paige stared at me, her eyes wide, her glow dimming. Then she flickered and swooped toward the floor.

"I'm sorry," I said quickly. I couldn't see her expression, but I didn't need to. I'd watched her trail Mom around the house. I'd been there every time she'd burst into my room, wailing, "She won't talk to me! Why won't she talk to me?" and thrown herself down onto the floor in a heap. That one fact took Paige forever to learn. I had a mom, and she didn't, not anymore.

"She's been away a long time, hasn't she?" Paige said. She glanced up at me, her eyes sunken into the shadows of her cheekbones. I could feel my arms hanging awkwardly at my sides. How could I comfort someone I couldn't touch?

"Yeah," I said. "Like usual. Dad said she'll be home on the weekend. It's on the calendar."

"Right. Like usual." Her lips smiled, but the rest of her face didn't.

Not that it would matter when Mom came back. She'd be just as far from Paige as now. As far as everyone living was, except me. I'd been so angry with Paige for pushing me out of her life back then, and now I was all she had. This wasn't exactly how I'd wanted it to be. Or what Paige would have chosen, if the lake had given her a choice.

"You know," I said, "I think this outfit needs something." I opened a couple dresser drawers, pawing through until I found it. A thin cotton scarf, sky blue, that Mom had brought back from Greece or Sweden or somewhere. Paige brightened as I looped it around my neck. I posed.

"How's that for color?"

I was sure it didn't go with the shirt, and I was sure Paige could tell, but she grinned anyway.

"Perfect."

She glided with me to the top of the stairs, and stopped. Dad was downstairs in the kitchen, chopping something for his breakfast omelet.

"See you," I whispered, and headed down to the front door.

Outside, everything smelled like dirt, making me wrinkle my nose. It'd rained again last night, and the air felt like a cool, damp towel against my skin. I hurried toward Frazer, trying not to think about the fact that I'd be stuck in the same building as Tim all day. So many opportunities for him to corner me. So many things that made me cringe when I tried to imagine discussing them with him. If he knew, if anyone else knew—what mattered was, how was I going to deal with it? Would it be better to deny everything?

I turned the corner and the school building came into sight. A troop of seniors had taken over the side stairs. They leaned against the railing, passing a joint from hand to hand. I hesitated at the edge of the lawn, suddenly unwilling to face anyone. Out of habit, my gaze drifted to the little ash tree that stood near the edge of the sidewalk. Its branches dipped in the breeze, the space beneath them empty.

If I squinted, I could almost make myself see Chester.

His back stiff and upright under his starched white shirt, his arms folded primly across a desk that wasn't there. Weird place to imagine a desk, but the ash tree had been his favorite spot. Every dead person seemed to have a place they liked best. They might leave it for a few hours now and then, but they never stayed away much longer. For Paige it was our house, for Norris the third floor of Frazer, for Bitzy the hall outside the gym, and for Chester, the front lawn, especially that tree.

He'd been a nice guy, Chester. He'd pick up all the parent gossip, hearing the murmurs exchanged in the cars as they dropped off their kids. I think he liked to pretend they were all his parents, too. Sometimes he'd even wander home with kids after school, but he'd never talk about what he saw. "Those things are meant to be private," he told me once, his thin face even more serious than usual, when we were sitting under the tree at lunch hour like we often did.

He had a lot of opinions about right and wrong that way, and he wasn't afraid to share them. It was kind of cool. The kids at Frazer, the living ones, could have learned a lot from him about honesty. From any of the dead, really.

Last June, he'd been here. In the summer, even, I'd wandered by a few times to shoot the breeze. But in September, I'd walked up to the tree on the first day of school, and he was gone. The faint smell of tea that had always hung in the air, even when he wasn't by the tree— that was gone, too. I hadn't seen him since.

I guess it made sense that the dead would go somewhere else, eventually. I mean, most people disappeared into the great unknown the second they stopped breathing. But he was the only dead person I'd known who'd been there and then not been.

Standing there on the school lawn, rubbing one of the leaves against my thumb, I felt my eyes go watery. I shook my head, trying to snap myself out of it. This wasn't the place to get weepy.

The seniors by the stairs started moving. One flicked the roach into the corner, and they all packed into the school. I sighed. I could handle whatever happened—I'd handled worse. My boots squelched in the muck as I walked over to the door. I pushed inside and headed downstairs.

The hall outside the gym was empty, but the usual early morning basketball practice was in full swing. The coach's shouts echoed through the doors, and balls pounded on the wooden floor. A girl bounded out of the gym and jogged to the water fountain, her face shiny with sweat. I walked past her, toward the pay phone alcove.

Bitzy shot through the wall like she'd been launched from a catapult. She spun around on one foot and followed with a plié. "I knew you were here," she said. "I just knew it."

I yawned, covering my mouth with my hand. "I'm here," I agreed. "Way too friggin' early."

"Well, I've got stuff to tell you." She put her hands on her hips and twisted at the waist one way and then the other. "Not so good as yesterday, of course, but hard to top that, right?"

"Right," I said, my mood lifting. The thing with Tim had thrown me so far off I'd almost forgotten how close I was to seeing Danielle's fall from grace. "So what's up?"

"Well, there was this guy—shaved head, nice muscles, wears a baseball jersey all the time? He was telling his friends—"

As she talked, a door whined open down the hall. Whoever was holding it paused and leaned against it, the sharp angle of a shoulder showing through the window. A female voice chirped, "Oh, I don't know. What do you think, Tim?"

I cut off Bitzy's sentence with a "shhhht." She leaned over to take a look.

"What?" she said, glimmering with curiosity.

"Never mind. I've got to go."

"But I didn't finish telling you!"

"I'll be back later, and we'll talk lots then. I promise."

"You'd better."

I cut through the cafeteria and headed up to my locker. My heart was pounding. Calm down, I told myself. It wasn't like he'd come racing through the school after me. Then the people whose opinions he cared about might see him.

I walked past the few freshmen already scattering the hall. The scent of Norris's hair oil hung in the air, but the kid himself was nowhere to be seen. Out watching track practice, I hoped. He'd remember about that for the next couple days, and then I'd have to remind him again. It could take a while to get something I could really use. Paul might have been just a few gropes shy of making it with Sharry, but now Danielle would be on red alert. He'd be steering clear of the equipment shed, I'd bet on that.

I opened my locker and stared at its contents. What classes did I have today, anyway? There was too much going on; I could hardly think. I closed my eyes and tried to push it all aside, if only for a moment.

Shoes squeaked on the linoleum around the corner. The soft, spaced footsteps of someone tall but light on his feet. I turned around.

Tim ambled around the bend, jerking to a stop when he saw me.

My options flitted through my head like leaves in a gust of wind. I could take off again. I could shut him down before he even got started. But . . .

I looked at him standing there awkwardly, his hands slung in his pockets, and all the snappy remarks I'd been forming died in my throat. Whatever Tim believed of the stuff people said about me, here he was in front of me, in the school this time, where people could see. I had to give him credit for that. If he wanted to take another stab at telling me what the hell he wanted with me, maybe I should give him a chance. I didn't have to say anything about me if I didn't think I could trust him.

"Hi," I said.

"Uh, hi." Tim swiped at the sprinkling of bangs that brushed his pale eyebrows. "I . . . look, I'm really sorry about yesterday. I didn't mean— It got a little crazy."

"Yeah, it did."

"Can we— Would you give me another chance to explain?"

"Sure. Spill away."

"No one's using the student council office right now," he said. "We can talk there."

I followed him down the hall and around the corner, past the classrooms, to the little side hall where the student council did its work. Tim pulled a key out of his pocket and unlocked the door. He held it open for me to step inside. There were a couple of couches and a coffee table between them, a computer on a desk in the corner, and a mini fridge beside it. I settled down on one of the couches, sweeping aside chip crumbs. Tim sat across from me. He leaned forward, his elbows resting on his knees.

"All right," I said, to get us on the right track, "so this is about your mom, right?"

For a few seconds, he lost his tongue. He inhaled, slowly.

"I guess you know, a couple months ago—"

"She died," I said, nodding. "What do you think that has to do with me?"

He looked at his hands, then up at me again. There was no trace of yesterday's smile. "I think," he said carefully, "that you know something about those books I was carrying. Is that right?"

I eyed him and said nothing. I'd agreed to listen, not to talk.

"So, I mean, can you do it? Like, contact the other

side? Or maybe you know a way, or you know someone who does. . . . I know it's not really my business, but . . . it's really important to me."

He sounded desperate. Really desperate. A feeling I could recognize. I ran my fingers along the edge of the coffee table, watching him.

"If there's some way I could talk to her," he continued, the words rushing out now, "contact her, see her, however it works, I'd do anything. I know it's a weird thing to ask. I just thought there was a chance that you might have some idea—"

I held up my hand, and his mouth snapped shut. So he hadn't seen her, hadn't heard her. He just wanted to. And he didn't know what I could do, just that I could do something psychic or magical, nothing specific, just enough for him to wonder.

I bit my lip. I could tell him I didn't know, that what I did had nothing to do with this, that he should just try whatever those books told him to do, and maybe it would work out. He missed his mom, and I was sorry for him, but he was also Tim Reed, VP. Tim who was good friends with Matti and Paul and Danielle and the rest of them. . . .

Something clicked, and the gears in my brain started whirring so fast I could almost hear them.

Tim would know things about Paul, about Danielle, things Norris and Bitzy might never stumble onto. This was the key to the vault, handed right to me. If I worked things right, I could have enough to show everyone—to show *Danielle*—just how far from perfect she was. And

Tim would get what he wanted at the same time. Both of us, happy. What kind of idiot would I be to pass on a chance like that?

I'd be the kind of idiot who'd rather keep a few things secret from the school VP.

"Have you told anyone?" I said.

His forehead crinkled. "Told?"

"About the contacting-the-dead thing."

He had the nerve to laugh. "Are you crazy? Tell people I'm trying to get in touch with my dead mother? Yeah, right."

Of course not. "I don't mean that," I said. "I mean about me."

"I haven't said anything about you."

"Not even a hint? Why do your friends think you're bugging me?"

"You think they know?" he said. "They wouldn't even care. Anyway, this has nothing to do with them. Look, I'm not going to say anything to anyone about any of this."

He had all the symptoms of sincerity, too: the clenched hands, the unblinking gaze, the defiant chin.

"We've got to be clear," I said. "If I do hear you've been talking about me, and I will hear if you do, you'll get the opposite of help. All right?"

He nodded.

"And I'll want you to do a few things in exchange." I hesitated and decided to leave it at that. He'd be more likely to let something slip about his friends if he didn't know what I was after.

"Sure," he said. "That's fair."

"I can't guarantee anything," I continued, measuring my words. "Do you have any reason to think your mom's stuck around?"

"I . . . I don't know."

"Well, I can't just snap my fingers. A lot of people are just gone, and that's that. There's a pretty good chance I'll find nothing."

"That's okay," Tim said, hope flickering in his eyes. "I just want to try."

I let out my breath. "As long as you're ready. She could have been the best mom ever and still have shot off to the next plane of existence without a second thought. They just do that."

Tim nodded, but his face shifted. The top part, around the eyes, started to sag, at the same time his mouth and jaw tensed up. That moment sealed the deal. I looked at him, and it was Paige all over again. Paige pulling that face four years ago, every time she'd screamed herself silly trying to get Mom to hear her. Paige making it this morning when she'd remembered Mom was away, again, as always.

Part of me said that Tim had no right to look that way, that lost. He had a dad, he had tons of friends, he had hope. If he had any clue what it was like, to really be left, the way Paige was, with no one but me and none of the people she wished she had . . .

But all of me knew that you couldn't fake that face. Not in a million years. Everything he'd said, he meant it.

"All right," I said. "I'm in. For now."

"Thank you," Tim said. "Really, thank you. I already have a bunch of stuff . . . obviously we can't do anything here." He twisted around on the couch and looked at the wall clock. I think he'd have dragged me off right then if he could have.

"Missing math will kill me, but I can skip the afternoon," he said. "Catch you at the beginning of lunch?"

I shrugged. If Mr. VP figured it was okay to cut a couple classes, I wasn't going to play the Goody Two-shoes. "Works for me."

CHAPTER 6

Two hours later, I was sitting in history class listening to Mr. Minopoplis lecture about the Civil War, and my stomach was churning in its own little rebellion. What the hell had I done? Tim had looked at me with his sad eyes and I'd agreed to help him—Tim, who had dozens of girls fawning over him, who could have had anything he wanted.

Except this. No one else could tell him if his mom had stuck around.

I probably should have just kept my mouth shut. What if I didn't find her? He'd be disappointed, maybe even angry, despite all his reassurances. Who was to say he wouldn't go running his mouth off about me then?

Even if I did find his mom, then what? What I knew about mother-son relationships could share the space on a single neuron with my understanding of steam engine maintenance. Probably I knew more about steam engines.

I'd tried to do it the other way around once. There'd been a girl hanging out by my junior high school, one of the first dead people I'd seen after Paige. I had no idea what I was doing, only that this kid kept bugging me to let her parents know she was still around, and it was driving me even crazier than I already felt. So I dug up her mom's e-mail address and tried to get in touch. The mom, unsurprisingly, was even less certain of my sanity than I was. She sent back a screaming message threatening to call the police on me if I mentioned her daughter again.

And look at Paige and Mom. Was I setting Tim up for something like that, knowing his mom was there but never being able to talk to her, to hear her acknowledge him?

I pressed the heels of my hands against my forehead. I had to get out of here, give myself a little time to think. It was almost lunchtime. I could probably get away with a puke run.

If you dash out of class with your hand over your mouth, teachers assume you're off to empty your guts into a toilet and will forgive you for not coming back. Especially if, like Mr. Minopoplis, they happen to know that you happen to know that they filched one of the school's TVs last year.

With the way my stomach was flip-flopping, I wasn't totally faking. I slid my arm into one of my shoulder straps and checked to see if Mr. M had noticed my preparations. He was busy writing a bunch of dates on the chalkboard. Jumping up, I swung my pack over my shoulder, clamped my hand to my mouth, and ran. I was out of the room before Mr. M even turned around.

I kept running until I got to the stairs, in case someone peeped out to see where I was going. Heading up to my locker, I slowed to a jog. My heart pounded against the tightness in my chest. When I got to the end of the hall, I closed my eyes and leaned my head against the cool steel. Sighing, I willed my body to relax.

Norris seeped out of the wall so close his jacket tingled through the side of my arm. "You're out early," he said.

I straightened up and opened my eyes. "Broke out of class."

"Cool." He hunched his shoulders, his jacket collar brushing his ears. "Something going down that I should know about?"

"Got a little field trip happening in a few minutes."

His eyes lit up. "Where're you going?"

"I'm not sure. I'm going on a ghost hunt for someone's dead mom, so we could end up just about anywhere."

I hefted my backpack, then chucked the whole thing in my locker. The afternoon was going to be hard enough without lugging that thing around. To hell with homework.

Norris floated around me. "A ghost hunt?" he said. "What for?"

"It wasn't my idea," I said.

"I guess not. Who is this someone, anyway?"

"Tim," I said. "You remember the note—and this morning . . ."

Norris stared at me. "Doesn't that guy have enough people doing favors for him? I thought he was near the top of the hit list."

"Well . . ." I scowled at my locker. "He kept bugging

me. And I figured I might get some dirt out of it. And anyway, it's not like anyone else can do this favor for him."

"Hey, if you think it's worth it. What are you going to do if you find her?"

"I don't know," I admitted. "I'm kind of hoping she didn't stick around." Chance, at least, was in my favor. If even a quarter of the people who'd died in this city had decided to hang around, I'd have been buried in them.

Norris shrugged. "Yeah, I bet she took off to the great beyond already. No worries."

He said it casually, but the bitterness crept into his voice anyway. Norris didn't know what the "great beyond" was any better than I did, and I doubted he cared that he was here and not there. It was the thing with his dad that bugged him.

My first year at Frazer, Norris spewed a lot of tough talk, like "I was getting beatings from the day I was born" and "That kid needs to be smacked around like I was." Making like he was better for it. His dad, I dragged out of him one day, was up at Summerlea General, and had been for a long time, with one of those diseases that takes its time killing you. Norris would disappear for a few hours every now and then to visit.

Then, last spring, I found Norris skulking in and out of the lockers, so dark I could have mistaken him for a shadow. "He died," he said. "The bastard finally died, and he didn't show up. He just left. He's gone." I guess he'd wanted to have one last chat with his dad, set some things straight. I think he'd been waiting for that. And he didn't get it.

Remembering that, I felt a jab of annoyance at Tim. Why should he get handed to him what everyone else had to do without? Death was supposed to be difficult. Life was supposed to be difficult. It'd figure if even death bent over for this guy.

"Just promise me you're not going soft on these kids," Norris said.

I laughed. "Not much chance of that."

"Good. It was a really long time before you came, Cass. I hardly remember it, but . . . I know it was boring as hell."

He dimmed as he said it, and I reached toward him without thinking. In a little more than a year I'd be out of here. But I didn't want to remind him of that.

"You want to come down to the parking lot?" I said. "I'm supposed to meet the grieving son at his car."

The glow came back to his eyes. "Sure. You got a plan?"

I thought it over as we drifted toward the stairwell. "Nah. Just could use the moral support."

"I bet I can do better than that."

We stepped out into the sunlight. The clouds had burned away, leaving the sky flawlessly blank. The parking lot stood to the right, four rows of rain-slicked cars surrounded by glinting puddles. I hopped over the guardrail between the lawn and the lot.

"It's the blue Oldsmobile," Tim had said. "You can't miss it." He was right. The Oldsmobile's boxy back end stuck out a foot farther than any other car's, and it had more dents than the cafeteria pop machine. It wasn't the usual car blue: deep, glossy, and royal. Nope, we're talking a pasty, pastel powder blue.

Tim was leaning against the trunk, which was so low he could have sat on it and kept his feet flat on the ground. He stood up as I walked over, and the car creaked. Norris floated along beside me, running his fingers longingly down the hood of a sleek convertible. He glanced at me, winked, and then dove into the Oldsmobile headfirst. He glided over to the trunk and hung there, his face immersed, like he was snorkeling in it.

The sun was on my side, so Tim had to squint to look at me. His hands seemed to be giving him a hard time. They jerked from his waist to an itch on his neck, refusing to stay still.

"Nice wheels," I said.

"It used to be my great-uncle's."

"Man, Cass, you wouldn't believe all the junk this dude's got," Norris shouted, lifting his head. "Let's see"— he plunged back in. "Lots of white candles. Incense. Matches. A big white sheet—looks like silk. Tape recorder. Nice mirror, all brassy. A couple photos. And a box of . . . tarot cards?"

My lips quirked. "Something funny?" Tim asked, shoving his hands into his jeans pockets.

I raised my eyebrows. "You brought enough stuff. Were you planning on holding a séance?"

Tim reddened. "What do you mean?"

"Candles, cards, personal effects. . . . Do you see me

carrying around any of that? Trust me, if you needed it, I'd have told you."

"Okay, okay," Tim said, flushing darker. "I didn't know. I thought I should get some things, in case. How did you—"

When I shrugged, he glanced back at the car, his eyebrows drawing together. Norris, sprawled on the trunk top, gave him a wave.

"You gotta mess with this guy a little, Cass," Norris said. "He's just asking for it. And I want to hear all about it tomorrow."

I gave him a brief nod. He wafted across the parking lot and through the bricks of the school's outer wall.

Tim ran his fingers through his hair. "So, uh, what do we do?" he said. "I mean, how are you going to find her? Or is it someone else, that you know?"

"It's just me," I said. "And I just look. Where'd she spend most of her time when she was alive—like, her free time?"

Tim answered quickly. "Home. I mean, she had friends and work—just part-time, but she liked being home more than anything."

He sounded sure. Good. There was some hope he wouldn't haul me off to half a dozen places if I didn't find her in the first spot, then.

"All right," I said. "That's where we'll go. Will it be clear there? No one home?"

"I think . . ." His eyes glazed for a second. "Yeah, that'll be okay. Let's go."

Playing gentleman, he opened the passenger-side door for me. I squeezed in. The inside of the car looked ten times smaller than the outside, all cramped gray leather. It smelled like Pine-Sol. Tim bent himself into the driver's seat, his legs grazing the bottom of the steering wheel. He backed out of the space fast and wide, and the bumper dinged the guardrail. That explained the dents.

As the car lurched out of the lot, Tim switched the radio on to some syrupy new-country station. He tapped the wheel in time with the music, but his fingers kept losing the beat. Just past the school, we hit a red light, and he glanced over at me.

"If she's there," he said, "at the house . . . will I be able to see her?"

I hesitated. We were getting closer and closer to the question of what exactly I could do. Well, he was going to find out soon enough, wasn't he?

"Probably not," I said. "How many people did you see in the parking lot?"

"Well, two: me and you. Oh." He blinked at the windshield, then looked back at me. "So . . . that's how you knew what I had? There was someone there?"

"You just said you didn't see anyone," I said, raising my knees so I could slide down in the seat. The ancient leather was soft and actually pretty comfortable.

"But, I mean, someone . . . dead. I don't know what you call them. A ghost, I guess?"

"If that's what you want to call them."

Tim grimaced. "I don't know. I think we've established that I don't have a clue about any of this."

"You act like you do," I pointed out. "I can buy that people at Frazer say all that spooky stuff about me. Not sure how you got from witches and psychics to talking to the dead, though. Or did you figure it'd be some kind of magic spell?"

The car behind us honked. The light had turned green. Tim looked away and hit the gas.

"There was something else," he said, staring at the road ahead. "When everyone started talking about you, after the thing with Paul yesterday, I remembered. This time, like a year ago, I skipped class and came out front, and you were sitting under that tree, the little one by the sidewalk, talking really quietly. You'd look over beside you like there was someone sitting there, but I couldn't see anyone."

My skin chilled. Had I really been that careless? Thank God it hadn't been a teacher who'd seen me, or I could have ended up back in therapy, or worse.

"It's not like I was sure," Tim kept going. "It just seemed worth a shot. I mean, obviously you can do something most people can't. It's not like there's anyone else I know where there's even a possibility. And even a little chance—"

"So why is it so important that you talk to her?" I asked. "She hide a winning lottery ticket before she died or something?"

"Is it so weird that I'd miss her?" Tim asked. His voice came out choked.

"No. But most people don't go to this much trouble trying to do something that's generally considered impossible." I tried to imagine Mom or Dad calling up TV psychics or getting books like Tim's out of the library. "Usually they just . . . accept."

"I guess I didn't realize until after she died that I was going to miss her so much." He paused. "Things started to change, people changed, after she got sick. Everyone looks at me differently, talks to me differently. It's like I never really knew them. If it had happened before, I'd have gone to her—she always knew how to deal with everything. She was always *there*. But obviously now . . . just knowing she's still here, if she is, I know it would make things better."

"Can't you just talk to your dad?" I asked. "It'd be a heck of a lot easier."

Tim was silent as he eased the car around the corner. "I can't," he said. "And it wouldn't."

He pulled up in front of a two-story house. "Well, here we are."

I peered up at the place through the window. Somehow, I'd expected a playboy mansion, with a huge deck and a hot tub for romancing the ladies, but it was a regular house, dull beige and navy-trimmed, with a couple of crooked shingles and a few scabs of paint flaking off the porch front. Just goes to show you can't believe teen television programming. Who knew—maybe Tim wasn't quite the brooding lady-killer, either.

I got out of the car before Tim could try to open the door for me. After he'd locked up, he stepped onto the sidewalk and looked at me like he was waiting for something.

"Oh," I said, catching the cue. "Nope, nobody out here."

"Okay."

I followed him up the steps to the front door. There was a little sign hanging on the porch wall, painted with autumn leaves and the word *Welcome* in flowery script. From the way Tim's eyes crinkled up when he saw it, his mom must have made it. My dad got the same look when he passed our mantel and saw the clay pony Paige had squished into shape in third grade. I guessed it didn't matter which of a zillion things you were grieving for, it'd cross your face the same way.

"Well, this is it," Tim said, pushing the door open. The front hall was dim. On the left, stairs rambled up to the second floor under a maroon runner. Through the narrow doorway on the right, a suede couch in matching maroon slumped in the shadows under a heavily curtained window. The only light, stark and artificial, came from the kitchen, straight ahead.

"He left the lights on," Tim muttered to himself. I heard him swallow. He gave me a smile, hard around the edges. "You want a drink?"

"No thanks."

I chucked my boots on the plastic shoe rack as Tim went on ahead. If we made the whole house as dark as the living room, finding a dead person should be a breeze. She'd stand out like a night-light. I skimmed over the stairs and banister, the side table with its vase of dried flowers, the shadowy shapes of furniture in the living room, and breathed deeply. The hall smelled like dusty leather. Unless Tim's mom had secretly been a dominatrix, I had the feeling that smell didn't come from her.

I walked into the harsh yellow glow of the kitchen. From the looks of things, no one had cooked there in ages. A row of gleaming pots dangled from a rack over the spotless stove. The counters and cupboards shone. A faint sweetness hung in the air, like a memory of cookies baked years ago.

The silence was starting to raise goose bumps on my arms. "She liked to cook?" I said, turning toward Tim.

"Nothing too complicated," Tim said. "She loved pies, though. She made an amazing lemon meringue."

He was taking a bottle of gin out of the freezer. It looked like water when he poured it into his glass, but it smelled sour. He topped it off with club soda and took a long sip.

So that was what he'd meant by a drink. It seemed a little early to start on the booze, but I wasn't about to lecture him.

"Nothing here?" he asked.

"Not on this floor."

"Where next—upstairs or down?"

"I'll check her bedroom first," I said, though really, anywhere other than that kitchen would have been fine. The fake brightness felt more haunted than the dark.

"Up," Tim said, and raised his glass to the stairs. He flicked a switch as we went down the hall. The kitchen light blinked out. "Dad wants to keep the lights off all the time to save on electricity," he said, like it was a bad joke.

The stairs creaked just a little less than the Oldsmobile,

which wasn't saying much. Upstairs the curtains were drawn back and sunlight warmed the rooms. Tim touched the door at the end of the hall. "This is her bedroom."

I poked my head in after him. The room looked lived-in: the ivory bedcovers rumpled, a shirt hanging from one of the dresser's brass knobs. A man's shirt. Of course. Tim's dad still slept in here.

"Mrs. Reed?" I said, stepping over the threshold. Tim sat on the bed, gingerly, and set his glass on the end table. Nothing else moved.

If Tim's mom were around, I'd have expected her to zip right over the second she heard her name. Actually, I'd have expected her to meet us at the door. Dead people aren't in the habit of hiding. It's the opposite, really—they follow the living all over the place. I mean, think about it:

1. Usually no one can see them anyway.
2. They're bored out of their minds, and breathers are the only things remotely entertaining.
3. If someone *can* see them, they're so excited to finally have someone to talk to that you're lucky if you can get them to shut up, ever.

With my head turned so Tim couldn't see, I let out a silent breath of relief. Looked like she was going to be a no-show.

I still had to act like I was looking, though, or Tim wouldn't be convinced. And I hadn't even tried any digging yet. I was here, I was doing what Tim had asked—he could return the favor.

"The way you talked about Paul yesterday, I guess he

must mess around a lot," I said, nudging open the closet. No moms in there. Just a whole lot of her clothes: whites and yellows and reds, the colors she'd filled the house with.

"I don't know. It's not like he tells me about it." Tim swiveled as I lifted the bed skirt. "So do you see any, like, signs? That she's around?"

"Not so far." All I saw under the bed was a heap of dust and a bunch of shoe boxes. I sneezed as I stood up. "But, I mean, you've heard stuff. About Paul."

Tim shrugged. "He's made a few comments when Danielle's not there, but it's hard to tell how serious he is. I guess Mom's not in here?"

"Nope."

"Let's try my room."

"Why not?"

Tim's bedroom hardly had space for his bed, which didn't leave many places for someone to hide. I picked up the framed photo from the computer desk that was squeezed between the foot of the bed and the wall. The little boy in it must have been Tim, aged six or so. Same light hair, same charming smile, a little rounder in the face. He was sitting on a woman's lap, and they were both resting on a blanket beneath a chestnut tree, paper plates and Styrofoam cups scattered around them. The woman, I guessed, was his mom. She had little Tim's head nestled in the arc of her neck and chin, and her honey-blond hair brushed his cheek. They were squinting, their faces bright with sun, and grinning at whoever was behind the camera. Tim's dad, probably. A happy family picnic.

Tim hovered at my side. "So, do you think—"

I shook my head. "Not looking so good," I said. "But there's still downstairs."

I pushed my hair back from my face, wondering if I could pull something out of Tim without being too obvious. Maybe if I started with something casual and general, like "What do you guys talk about all lunch hour, anyway?" and ran with whatever he gave me.

I was working out the wording and turning toward the doorway when I saw her.

It was just a face, emerging out of the wall, pale and framed by golden hair. Her gray-blue eyes met mine. The delicate eyebrows drew together, the lips parted, and then she jerked back into the wall so quickly it left me dazed and blinking. My breath stuck in my throat.

"What, what is it?" Tim asked. He leaned past me to see where I was looking.

"I don't know." It had been too fast. I couldn't be sure if it was the woman in the photo. I went to the door, glanced up and down the hall. Whoever it had been, she'd made a dash for it as soon as she'd realized I could see her. Weird.

But she'd left something behind. As I breathed, I caught the scent, light and sweet like powdered sugar. The sweetness in the kitchen—it'd been her. I bent over the railing, and it grew stronger.

"Well, let's go," Tim said. He bounded down the first few steps, then hesitated and looked up at me. "I mean, it's okay, right? Or should we wait? Do you think she's nervous?"

"I don't even know if it's your mom," I said, feeling

uneasy. What was with the game of hide-and-seek? I'd come as a huge favor to her son—if it was her—and she took off on me?

"Go ahead," I told Tim. I hurried down behind him, catching up at the bottom of the stairs. The hall was as still and empty as before. I stared into the dark rooms, frowning. The sugary smell was fading. In a few minutes, it would be just a subtle undertone, so faint I'd almost missed it coming in because I hadn't known to look for it.

I marched into the living room. Dust whirled. The sofa, the TV cabinet, the dark-stained hardwood gave no hint of her. I brushed past the chairs around the dining room table, and there—a wisp of blond hair and white dress, vanishing into the kitchen; the taste of powdered sugar on my tongue. I tore around the table and through the doorway. The figure slipped through a closed door just beyond the edge of the counter.

"That way," I said with a jab of my finger. "Can we go?"

"Sure. It's just the basement."

I grabbed the knob and pulled it open as Tim came up behind me. He touched my arm.

"What's going on?" he said. "It's like we're chasing her. Is she running away?"

"Don't worry about it," I said, even though that was exactly what we were doing. Why didn't she want me to see her? Was there some page in the ghost etiquette book I'd missed, some way I'd broken the rules, offended her? I hurried down the steps. Above me, Tim flicked on the basement light. My socked feet cold on the concrete floor, I circled the laundry room, stopping once to peek inside the washing machine. Tim strode past me, heading for a door in the paneled wall.

"Maybe the rec room?"

The door opened for him.

"I thought I heard someone upstairs." A man leaned out, glancing at Tim and then me. He rubbed his broad nose and the bristly mustache beneath. "Well. You brought a new friend."

Tim had gone stiff, his hands clenched behind his back. "Dad," he said in a tight voice. "You're home early."

"So are you."

"Early dismissal," Tim replied, so smoothly I'd have believed him if I hadn't known he was lying. "Anyway, we were just leaving."

Tim's dad gave him a long look. His eyes were round and droopy, like a basset hound's. Then he nodded. "Nice to meet you," he said to me, and vanished back into the rec room.

Tim spun around and stomped up the stairs, but I hung back. She'd gone in there, with his dad, I was sure. She'd known we wouldn't follow.

Why wouldn't she want to talk to me? It didn't make sense. Unless I really had done something wrong, without meaning to.

I swallowed thickly and headed upstairs.

"Of all the rotten luck," Tim was grumbling when I reached the kitchen. His face softened, just a bit, when he saw me. "Sorry. If I'd known he'd be home, I wouldn't have wasted your time."

Technically, it was the dead person who'd wasted my

time, but I'd rather Tim thought I had everything under control.

"This is an old house," I said. "It might not be her. Could be someone from ages ago." I paused. "Turn on the light?"

Tim pushed the switch and looked at me expectantly. I looked back at him. Even in the yellowy light, his eyes were a cool gray-blue. The same as hers. I dropped my gaze and let my hair fall over my face.

"I'll get going," I said.

"Sure, of course." Tim sounded nervous all of a sudden. Wondering what I'd seen inside his head, maybe. "You live far? I could drive you."

"It's just over on Earl Street," I said. "I'll walk."

"Well . . . here." He grabbed a pad of paper and a pen from the hall table and jotted something down. "My cell number. Just in case you think of anything, or—"

I nodded, and stuffed it into my pocket.

I expected a million questions as I laced up my boots, but he was silent, leaning against the stair railing. When he saw me out, he said, "Thank you," instead of goodbye, in a voice like I'd donated him a lung. Didn't ask whether I was coming back to try again, or if I thought next time we might find her. He must have been thinking it. I guess he was scared I'd say no if he pushed.

The thing was, even I wasn't sure how I would answer when he did.

CHAPTER 7

Our next-door neighbors, the Guzmans, had this enormous gray van that as far as I could tell never left their driveway. It totally hid our house from anyone coming up on the west side. So it wasn't until I trudged past it that I saw Paige out on our front lawn and stopped dead in surprise. She was drooped over the lazy-man's garden Mom had thrown together on one of her brief visits home, skimming her hand through the tulips and daisies, so dim her hair and face blurred together.

I glanced up and down the street. Nothing moved except the sparrows swooping between the Stevensons' red maple and Mr. Bradley's oak. No one living hung out on Earl Street at two in the afternoon.

Paige flopped onto her back and lay there with her arms folded over her chest, three feet above the ground. If she was trying to freak me out with her corpse impression, she was doing a good job.

"Hey, Paige," I said, scooting closer so I could talk quietly. "What's going on?"

"Cassie?" Paige murmured. She didn't bother to look over.

"No, the masked avenger."

She didn't smile, either.

With a loud sigh, she rolled onto her side. She looked at the locks of hair that fell across her arm and started twisting one of them between her fingers.

"Do you think Larry still remembers me?" she said.

Oh, no. It'd been so long since the last time she'd gone mopey about Larry, I'd thought she was over it.

"Sure he does," I said, trying to sound so convincing that I wouldn't have to elaborate. Larry would have forgotten his last name before he forgot Paige. Watching a rescue team haul your dead girlfriend's body out of the bottom of a lake is one of those things that'll stick with you. But I didn't think that was quite the way Paige wanted to be remembered.

Paige murmured incoherently and threw herself down with her face buried in her arms. I crouched down on the grass beside her. "Hey, Paige, of course he remembers you. You remember all the guys you dated, right? And you and Larry went out for, like, a year."

"Yeah," Paige said. "But boys are different."

"Not that different. Nobody forgets you, Paige."

She peeked at me over her arm, her eyes huge and dark in her hazy face.

"What's with you today?" I asked. "Why are you worrying about Larry?"

She hesitated. "I went to his house," she said. "I just, y'know, wanted to see how he's doing. And—"

"And?" I braced myself for the worst. Sometimes Paige didn't know when to leave things alone. It'd been a nightmare when she'd caught him banging one of her former friends a month after the funeral. Thank God for her awful after-death memory, or she'd still be in hysterics over it.

"He's gone!" Her voice quavered. "All his stuff . . . his whole room, it's empty, his mom was in there repainting. I don't know where he went."

"Oh," I said. "Well, he'd be twenty-one now, wouldn't he? He must have moved out, got an apartment somewhere. Maybe he's going to college out of state. I'm sure he's okay."

Paige stared at me. "College," she said. Which was where she'd have been, if she hadn't . . .

"Never mind," I said, too loud. A blackbird shuddered off the phone line overhead. "It's no big deal. Let's go inside. I'll watch some TV with you."

"No," Paige whined. "No, no, no." She squashed her face into her arms, her shoulders shaking. As far as I know, the dead can't produce tears, but that didn't stop Paige from going through the motions of crying. "I want Mom," she said. "Where's Mom?"

Where was Mom? Mom was jetting off around the world just to avoid thinking about Paige. I'd been the one here with Paige through every tragedy she'd wailed over for the last four years. Didn't that count?

Even in that flash of anger, I knew it didn't. Paige's last night, four years ago, it'd been Mom fluttering around her, giggling with her and touching up her hair. I knew, because I'd heard them through the wall between Paige's bedroom and the bathroom, where I'd been perched on the edge of the bathtub, ripping threads out of a hand towel. I'd gone and thrown myself onto my bed in the dark, and hated Paige for having everything, for not noticing what was happening to me at school, for not caring— hated her so much I'd wished she'd disappear and never come back.

Guilt swelled in my stomach. "She'll be home soon," I said. Not that Paige would get any comfort when Mom returned. What had she done, back then, when Paige was upset? I couldn't replicate the hugs or the soothing voice. Even if Paige would have liked a root beer float, she couldn't drink one now.

The breeze rose, wisping across my face, and I smelled Mom's daisies and the rosebush next door. Flowers. That'd been one of their rituals: Mom and Paige strolling over to the flower shop, picking out the best bouquet, and splitting it between the dining room table and Paige's desk. Nothing got Paige beaming like a vaseful of fresh flowers to bury her face in.

I shoved my hands into my pockets. A buck-fifty snack money. I'd spent most of the week's allowance at the Salvation Army store buying these stupid boots.

Hell, it was spring. Any idiot could find flowers for free. A little surprise to cheer Paige up—I could manage that.

"Go inside," I told her. "Hang out with Dad. I'll be back in a bit."

Paige drifted upright. "Dad's gone to a lunch meeting with a client."

"Well, hang out in there anyway. My radio's on, isn't it? Listen to some music. I'll be back in half an hour, tops."

"All right," she said, her voice heavy with melancholy, and wafted toward the porch.

I jogged around the house to grab the old bike from the garage. As I came back up the driveway, Paige was just vanishing into the wall. I hopped on the bike and coasted onto the road, making it past five houses before I had to start pedaling. At the corner, I turned left onto Mabel Avenue. Six blocks up, the yard of Rockefeller PS, my old elementary school, bordered on a city park. The parks crew only bothered to mow the lawn every month or two, and most of the time they missed the edges.

As I braked outside the playground, the wheels squeaking, Melvin was making his usual rounds. He was a strange old guy with bushy eyebrows and a floppy mustache, so dim he'd have faded into the scenery if it weren't for his brilliant yellow suit. He was the only dead person I'd met who was always wandering, sometimes in the school yard, sometimes outside the strip mall a few blocks over, sometimes on the street right past my house.

I called him Melvin in my head because he looked like a Melvin, but I had no clue what his real name was. The one time I'd tried to start up a conversation, he had poked at me with his cane and sputtered something about the "corruption of a decaying metropolis crumbling on the heads of the masses." I'd pretty much left him to himself after that.

Now he swung his cane like a golf club as he walked

past me, whacking it through the chain-link fence that surrounded the tennis courts to the left of the school yard. I nodded to him, and he narrowed his eyes. When he'd moved on, I leaned my bike against the fence and shuffled along the edge of the tennis courts. The grass there, shot through with sprigs of wild violets, clover, bluebells, and Queen Anne's lace, brushed my calves. I kneeled and started picking.

After a few fumbles, I found a system: Pick with the right hand, hold with the left. I plucked a bunch of everything but the dandelions, which to Paige were more weeds than flowers. When I got to the end of the fence, my fingers were tacky with brownish-green sap. I went back to the playground and stopped by the wooden ramp of a slide to evaluate my bouquet. The colors and shapes jumbled together in a florist's nightmare, but the bunch was big and bright. It smelled sweet when I lowered my nose to it. I held it out in front of me, eyeballed it, and decided it would do.

Behind me, up on the paved area just outside the school, shoes started slapping the pavement in time with the thudding of a basketball. The net swished. I sat down on the grass, setting the flowers in my lap. The trick would be getting them home on the bike without losing the petals on the way. I pulled at the hem of my shirt, trying to figure out if I could swaddle them in it without flashing random passersby. It'd work if I kept a hand on them. Leaning against the side of the ramp, I started to stand up.

A coy, ever-so-slightly nasal voice floated to me from across the distance. "Waiting for someone?" I hesitated, still half crouched. It was a voice I knew. The basketball hesitated, too.

"Hey there, gorgeous," said another familiar voice. "I was wondering if you were ever going to get here."

I sidled around and peered over the top of the ramp. Danielle and Paul were standing entwined on the pavement near the school entrance, her hair falling over his manly biceps. They were going at it so enthusiastically you could tell they were using their tongues even from where I sat. Good thing the little kids hadn't gotten out yet—their innocent minds would have been scarred for life.

It'd been so long since I'd hung out at Danielle's place, it hadn't even occurred to me that she lived close to Rockefeller Elementary. Her house was half a block off Mabel; you could see the top of the school building from her parents' bedroom window. We used to wander over after school, grab some cookies from the kitchen, and prance Barbies around her bedroom. Back when we were the innocent kids.

Danielle stepped away from Paul, smacking the ball out from under his arm. She laughed as he lunged after it.

"Foul play!" he called, scooping it up. "Free throw for the home team." He leaned over for another game of tonsil hockey. I eyed the gravel and fought the urge to gag.

After a century or two, they pulled apart. "I had to hand in that late essay to Ms. Corning," Danielle said, breathless. "I swear she was hiding from me. I went all over Frazer looking for her. So you coming over? My parents won't be home until six."

"Now, that's an invitation I can't refuse," Paul replied. "You don't need to pick up your brothers?"

"They're going over to a friend's place today," she said. "It's just us."

"That's the way I like it." He tucked his free arm around her shoulders, and they meandered off the pavement and across the field.

I slumped against the pine boards of the ramp. Fat lot of good my words yesterday had done. Of course, Danielle thought I was dog dirt, so why should she care what I said? And Paul could be pretty slick, I guess. He'd probably convinced her I was making things up to get to her. I hadn't given any details, any names. Pretty easy to imagine it all away. The last couple years she'd had no shortage of practice ignoring me.

"Bitch," I muttered. The flowers rustled as I clenched my hands. She was supposed to be stewing over it. Going sour as she tried to figure out what he'd done. But no, nothing could stop Miss Danielle Perry from being sweet as cheap table syrup. To everyone but me.

I lowered my head, breathing in the scent that now smelled cloying. Was it going to do any good, anyway, if I forced her to face the facts? Would it really make up for everything she'd done?

No. Of course not. But that wasn't the point. The point was, she needed to realize how it felt to be slapped in the face by someone you counted on. To have everyone think—no, know—she'd deserved it. If she got just one taste, in some small way, we'd be even.

I got up, my legs wobbly. I hadn't lost yet. I still had

the details and the names. I could get more. Norris and Bitzy were on the lookout, and I'd hardly gotten started with Tim. Maybe I'd have to tell him straight out what I wanted. He hadn't seemed like he cared much about Paul. Hell, he might even approve. He'd already surprised me a couple times.

From inside the school, the bell dinged. Any second, the yard was going to be flooded with little kids. I hurried to my bike. Bundling the flowers inside my shirt, I cradled them with my arm. Then, steering one-handed, I took off for home.

CHAPTER

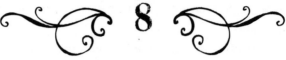

8

Paige beamed when I showed her the flowers and hovered all evening near the vase I set on my dresser. She even pecked me good night with an airy kiss on my cheek. But when I woke up the next morning to the shrill beeping of my alarm, she was off sniffling under the desk.

She puttered around my room as I dressed for school, skipping all her usual complaining about my choice of clothes, just twirling her hair and sighing. When I asked her what radio station she wanted, she just shrugged. "Whatever. It doesn't matter."

I poured a cup of fresh water into the vase. The flowers were already wilting.

By the time I headed out the door, I felt like the word *inadequate* was carved into my forehead. Finding Tim standing on our porch steps didn't improve my mood.

"Hey," he said, when I stopped on the doorstep and stared at him. He wavered, squinting up at me. His face was sallow everywhere but the smudges under his eyes.

"Hey," I said back. Behind him, the Oldsmobile was parked on an angle in the driveway. One of the back tires had gouged the edge of the lawn.

Tim followed my gaze. "Oh. Sorry. I'm off my game today. Rotten headache." He rubbed his forehead and made his painful smile at me. "I'll be better with some coffee in me. I thought . . . uh, my dad's heading off to work—not for a half hour or so, but I wanted to catch you before you got to school. So I'll buy you breakfast and then we'll try again?"

"Everything all right, Cassie?" Dad called from upstairs.

"Yeah, no problem." I stepped down onto the porch and let the door swing shut. "How'd you find my house?" I asked Tim.

"Well, you told me you're on Earl Street," he said. "There aren't that many McKennas in the phone book."

For a guy who had claimed not to be a stalker, he sure knew the tricks of the trade.

"So, are we going?" Tim said, shifting from foot to foot.

"I'm supposed to be going to school," I reminded him. "And I'm pretty sure you are, too."

"You didn't have a problem skipping yesterday."

"Well, you should give a person a little warning before you show up wanting to drag them off somewhere. You make it seem like you snap your fingers and I'm supposed to jump."

He swallowed audibly. "I . . . I didn't mean, I just thought . . ."

"Never mind." I wasn't that annoyed at him. It was just another crack in a day that felt like it was falling apart before it'd even started.

So he wanted me to go back to his place, to find the

woman who didn't want to let me so much as see her. I remembered yesterday's chase—the way she'd slipped away, fleeing from me—and my chest tightened.

My mouth started to form a no, but I caught myself in time. Don't think about that. Think about Danielle. I did this for Tim, whether his mom ran from me or decided to talk, and I could ask for that one thing in return. That would be fair, wouldn't it? That would make it worth it.

"If I keep helping you," I said, "I need you to do something for me. All right?"

"Sure," Tim said. "Whatever. I mean I said I would, just tell me whatever you want."

This wasn't the sort of discussion I wanted Dad to overhear. And Tim looked about ready to topple down the steps.

"How about you get yourself that coffee and we'll talk about it when you're conscious."

He started to laugh and winced. "I like that plan."

"All right." I eyed the car. "Just so you know, I'm walking."

"Yeah, that's not a bad idea. I think I saw a coffee shop around the corner. It's okay if I leave the car parked here?"

"Sure. It'll help my dad track you down if you decide to kidnap me along the way."

The only trouble with walking was Tim couldn't take a step or two without wincing and holding his head. It should have taken two minutes, but with him it was ten. "Why don't you take some painkillers or something?" I said as we finally reached the Café De Lite's door.

"Already did," Tim said. "Don't worry. An espresso works miracles."

I guess Mr. Drinks-Gin-at-Noon knew what he was talking about. We sat at a spindly-legged table on the concrete patio, me with a mochaccino and a blueberry muffin and him with his espresso, and his color improved by sips. When I made it to the bottom of my mug, he was already on his second and perky as could be.

"Okay," he said. "I am one hundred percent awake now. So what was it you wanted?"

I gulped down a mouthful of muffin and decided to just throw it out there. "Everything you know about Paul—and Danielle. All of it."

He cocked his head. "Can you be more specific? I can tell you Paul's birth date, or Danielle's favorite color, but I don't think that's what you're looking for."

That was a better reaction than I'd hoped for. He seemed cool with it, just cautious. Maybe Tim wasn't so bad, at least when you could do something he wanted.

"Stuff most people wouldn't know," I said. "Stuff the two of them wouldn't *want* most people to know. Even if it's just something you heard, and you don't know for sure. It's all good."

"And I guess this is for more of that vigilante stuff you do."

"Yeah, you could say that."

He turned the cup in his hands, making the foam swirl. "You know, Paul and I aren't so close. Maybe we used to hang out more, but even then . . . it's not like we talk about a lot of deep secret stuff. Why him and Danielle, anyway?"

"Danielle and I go back," I said. "I owe her a few."

"So this isn't about the good of the world at large. It's personal."

I stiffened. "I think the world at large benefits from having people's crap brought out in the open. So are you going to help me?" I started to stand up. "'Cause if not, I do have a class to get to."

"Hey, sit down," Tim said. "It's not that big a deal. I'd pick Mom over any of them any day. And I guess I already owe you for yesterday."

I sat, and folded my arms on the table, ready to listen. Tim set down his mug.

"What I know about Paul . . . he makes a lot of jokes about messing around with other girls, but I don't think he really has, not for a while. Never mentioned anyone or any time specifically." He paused. "He did start calling his car the lovemobile, so maybe he's got something going on there."

"What kind of car?"

"Mustang GT," Tim said. "Red. Coupe, not convertible. He usually parks it down the street instead of in the school parking lot. Afraid some careless student driver like me will smash it."

"Well, that's something." I'd have to tell Norris and Bitzy to keep an eye on that car. Who knew what he'd been getting away with out there? "Anything else? It doesn't have to be girl stuff."

Tim considered, nudging the mug in a slow circle with his thumb.

"Other than Danielle, and the joking, all he really talks about is sports. He's on the basketball team and the track team—you probably already know that. Um, he was pretty pissed about not making the athlete of the year list, since this is his last year at Frazer."

My lips quirked.

"What?" Tim said. "That's good?"

"I just know a few things Paul doesn't." Like that he'd originally been on the nominations list. Like which of his friends had gotten him scratched off. "So how about Danielle?"

"Not much to tell there. I mostly only see her when it's a bunch of us together. She's going to run for student council next year, she says, and she had some job at the mall that fell through. She seemed upset about that. Otherwise"—he shook his head—"that's all I've got. Honestly, yeah, she talks kind of harsh sometimes, but I've also seen her do stuff like spend her lunch hour helping some girl she barely knows get a stain out of her shirt."

Naturally Danielle showed off her generous spirit when people who counted were around to see. I raised my eyebrows. "That's it? You spend all that time with those guys—"

Tim grimaced, and I felt a tiny hiccup of guilt. Then, slowly, a hint of a smile crept across his face. It made me more uncomfortable than the grimace had.

"You know," he said, "there's a party at Matti's place

tomorrow night. I wasn't planning on going, I see enough of those guys as it is, but if you came—"

"Me? A party?" The closest thing to a party I'd been to in four years was that last junior high dance, when every girl refused to stand within five feet of me and the boys took turns blowing spitballs at me and muttering lewd comments as they brushed by. "But . . . I— They wouldn't even let me come in, would they?"

"Sure, if you came with me." He looked at me curiously. "I figured you could scope out all the gossip you wanted. And I wouldn't be stuck with only them for company. But it's not like you have to. It was just an idea."

Great, now he thought I was chicken. I gritted my teeth. What was my problem? It'd be spectacular. All the biggest poseurs in one house, getting drunk and stoned, defenses down. I could clear up more crap in one night than I had all year.

And still my heart was making nervous patters at the base of my throat.

"I'll consider it," I said.

"You should come," he said, his smile growing. "It would be . . . interesting, anyway."

A shop attendant shuffled over and gathered our mugs. "You want anything else?" Tim asked.

"Nah, I'm ready to get out of here."

He hesitated. "So, ah—my place?"

A thought raced through my mind: I had all he could give me, I could walk off without looking back, without having to deal with this dead person who wanted nothing to do with me. As fast as it had come, I shook it away. Tim had done his bit, and I'd be as full of crap as the rest of them if I skipped out on mine.

"Why not?" I said. Relief washed over his face so fast I almost thought he'd start bawling. "I'll do what I can," I added quickly. "She was a little . . . shy, last time. I can't promise this'll work out."

"Hey," Tim said, raising his hands, "I'm not picky. I'll take whatever you can get. You trust me to drive now?"

"I guess." I trusted him enough that I'd rather risk five minutes in the car than walking with another half hour of awkward conversation.

Naturally, Tim managed to work in a whole heap of awkwardness anyway. "If you don't mind me asking," he said, pushing back his chair to get up, "about the spirits and stuff. How's that work? You just see them? Since always?"

My throat closed up, and I turned away as I stood so he couldn't see my face. My fingers mashed the last few crumbs of muffin into powder. "Yes, I see them," I said. "No, I haven't always." Only since the morning after Paige's junior prom.

I'd replayed the memory so many times that it ran like a movie in my head. That night, I'd stayed up into the wee hours listening for the click of the door and the shuffle of Paige's shoes in the hallway, then woken up late and groggy in the morning, realizing I'd drifted off without meaning to. When I'd plodded past Paige's half-open door to the stairs, she was there. I only got a glimpse of her, curled up on her bed, wailing so loud I thought they must have been able to hear her down the street. Nothing new. Some tragedy at the prom, I figured—Larry had broken up with her, or kissed some other girl, or she'd spilled punch on her gorgeous dress. Odd that Mom wasn't in there comforting her, but maybe Paige had been inconsolable. It had happened before.

Then I reached the bottom of the stairs and heard Mom sniffling in the dining room. My skin started prickling. Mom never cried, not where anyone could see her. Where was Dad? Panic hit me, and I bolted into the dining room.

Dad was there, standing behind Mom, squeezing her shoulders. Mom swiped at her eyes with a tissue.

"Oh, Cassie," she said.

Dad took over. "Cassie"—his voice creaked—"your sister—"

What? Paige was sick? Hurt? But she'd be okay, she always was.

He cleared his throat. "Your sister . . . died last night."

I stared at them. The words hit me and stuck. They couldn't quite wriggle into my head. Mom and Dad were wrong. Paige wasn't dead. She was upstairs. I'd just seen her—hadn't I just seen her?

"Cassie," Mom murmured.

I fled, back up the stairs to Paige's door, and peered inside. There she was. Sobbing, quietly now, into her pillow. I pushed open the door, gearing up to tell her to get her butt downstairs and sort things out, and that was when I noticed. The edge of the pillow, the rose-print sheets, they showed right through her. She sat up as the door tapped the wall, and I could see the maple head-board through her pink-tinged face.

"Cassie?" she said. "Cassie, everyone's crazy! They won't talk to me; they won't even look at me. Can you ask Mom what's wrong? I can't get her to tell me—"

I welcomed my newfound talent by yanking the door shut and running straight into my closet, where every-thing was dark and solid, and nothing outside seemed real. I did it, I kept thinking, I wanted her gone, and now she is. To everyone but me. I did this.

"Cass? Hey, Cass?" Tim was saying. I jerked my head up. We were at the corner of Earl Street—somehow I'd arrived there.

"I was just thinking," I said.

"Yeah, I noticed." He ducked his head. "I mean, I'm sorry I asked, I didn't mean to—"

"It's fine. You wanted to know when it happened. Four years ago. Right after my sister died. The how part, I don't know. It didn't come with a manual."

I pushed my hair behind my ears and started walking toward my house so briskly I left Tim behind. After a second, he caught up.

"Wow," he said. "Must have been rough. I'm sorry about your sister. Do your parents know?"

I sputtered a laugh. "What do you think? I was so freaked at first that I tried to tell them, and that just got me sent to a shrink. Far's they know, it was a brief, grief-stricken episode that will never repeat itself." There were some things parents weren't built to handle. Having a twelve-year-old daughter babbling that she can see her sister's ghost must be one of them.

At the car, Tim unlocked the passenger door first. I wanted to sink into the seat and lean my head against the window, but not with Tim watching. He was already looking at me funny. I had to pull myself together.

"What's it to you, all that stuff, anyway?" I said.

"It's interesting." He turned the key in the ignition, and the engine coughed. "I don't meet a whole lot of people who talk to the dead, you know. Do you . . . are there other things, too, that you—"

"I can look for your mom. That's all that's important to you, isn't it? I'm not a walking freak show."

"I don't think you're a freak."

"Right."

"Well, I don't." He paused for a second to check his blind spot as he eased out of the driveway. "*Interesting* and *freak* aren't the same thing. My mom used to say, 'Every person you meet's like a fascinating story you've never read before.'"

"That's real wise," I said.

"I don't know if she was wise," Tim said. "But she was . . . good. If you needed her, she'd drop everything. She was always there. That's more than I can say for anyone else I know."

"Must have been nice. And it was just you, no brothers or sisters?"

He nodded. "She said every family she knew with

more than one kid, the parents always ended up playing favorites, even if they didn't mean to. She didn't want that to happen."

Well, I could back her up on that one. "So she was good and selfless and all—didn't she do anything for herself?"

"It was for her. She really liked helping, being there for people—she worked at the seniors' home, volunteered at the homeless shelter around the holidays. Is it so hard to believe someone would *want* to do all that?"

I shrugged. "It's hard to believe she didn't have anything that was just for her."

"Well . . ." His eyes went distant as he scanned the road. "She liked music. I used to come home and she'd be singing along to some oldies album. And she took piano lessons for a while. I think the keyboard's still in the basement. . . ."

His voice halted, and I remembered what—or rather, who—we'd come across in that basement yesterday.

"Since we're talking about fascinating stories," I said, "what about this thing with you and your dad?"

Tim slammed on the brake just in time for a stop sign, jolting me against the back of my seat. As he waited for the other car to make its left turn, he flexed his fingers against the wheel.

"What do you mean?" he said, his voice hardening.

"I'm not blind. Yesterday you looked like you'd rather stab him than say hello. And you told me yourself you couldn't talk to him."

"Yeah, well, I don't want to talk *about* him either, okay?"

"You think I live to share stories about how I see dead people?"

"Just leave it alone," he snapped.

I tipped my head back and looked up at the faded gray of the car ceiling. "Whatever you say."

The car puttered forward, Tim staring grimly ahead. Figured. It was like that day at the park, all over again. He was all gung-ho to hear about the freaky parts of my life, but a little question about his family issues—

"He left," Tim said, suddenly. He stopped, and I waited. "When Mom got sick, and we knew she wasn't going to get better, he couldn't take it. Said it was too hard for him, watching her get weaker . . . so he took off. The hospital moved her back home toward the end, and he moved out. Stayed in a motel somewhere. I didn't see him for months. He only came back when she was in the hospital again for the last few days. Okay?"

My mouth fell open, but it was empty. I had no words for that.

"He— You were on your own?" I managed.

"Well, there was a nurse in ten hours a day, and my aunt, my mom's sister, spent a lot of nights. It helped having her there."

"What a jerk. You must hate him."

Tim said nothing, his eyes fixed on the windshield. A streak of cloud was sliding in from the lake, white with a gray belly. He took the turn onto his street smoothly and parked outside his house in silence.

I took a deep breath. After that whole conversation-turned-confessional, I felt as wrung out as a dishcloth.

Time to snap out of it, focus. Tim's mom couldn't escape into the basement this time, but nothing would stop her from sinking into the walls or floating up through the roof. Maybe I had done something to scare her off yesterday, but she wouldn't remember me today, anyway. Maybe she was just scared of people in general. I had to assume, no matter what I did, she might not stick around long once I got inside. I'd have to start pitching my case the second I walked in the door.

"I think you should stay outside for now," I said to Tim. "Give me a chance to explain things to her."

Tim frowned. "You can't explain with me there?"

"If she's nervous, the more people there are, the harder it'll be to get her to listen. Soon as she's ready, I'll shout for you."

"Okay." Getting out of the car, Tim glanced up at the house, his mouth tight. "But as soon as you can—"

"Of course," I said. "What have I got to talk to her about?"

I waited by the car while he loped down the driveway to check the garage. "He's definitely gone," he yelled back to me. "We're good to go."

We walked up to the porch, and he handed me his keys. "Go ahead. It's the big silver one. I'll wait here."

I jingled through the keys until I found the one I needed. The lock stuck for a second, then clicked. The door drifted open.

"Mrs. Reed?" I called, hopping over the doorstep into the darkness of the hall. A wisp of powdered sugar lingered beneath the dust. I dropped the key ring onto the shoe rack, shoved the door shut with my foot, and lowered my voice. "Mrs. Reed, I need you to come out for a minute, for Tim. I know you can hear me, and if you'll talk to me I can hear you, too. It's just for Tim, I promise. I think he wants to know that you're . . . okay, or something. Now that he thinks you're here, I don't think he's going to give up, so let's get it over with, all right?"

The taste of sugar tingled on my tongue, and the living room brightened, faintly. I stepped through the doorway. "Mrs. Reed?"

The dining room was filled with an airy glow, and inside the glow a woman floated. Her white summer dress rippled around her willowy body. She glided toward me, stopping on the threshold with her hands clasped in front of her. Beneath the curls of her honey-blond hair, her face was thin and wan. She stared at me with eyes the same gray-blue as Tim's.

She was the prettiest dead person I'd ever seen. If I hadn't known better, I might have thought she was an angel.

"Who are you?" she said, her voice mild but uneasy.

I exhaled slowly. "I'm . . . sort of a friend of Tim's. We both go to Frazer. He asked me to come."

"Why? What do you want?"

"I don't want anything," I said. "It's Tim, it was his idea. He just wants . . . well, I don't know exactly what he wants, but I think he'd like to talk to you, knowing you're here. He's waiting outside. Will you stay here if I go get him?"

Her forehead creased. "This isn't a good idea. You shouldn't have let him—"

"Hey, wait a sec." I held up my hands. "I didn't 'let him' anything. I'm only here because he made me come. Your son's a stubborn guy, you know."

She dimmed, the shadows seeping through her. "I know," she said. "I'm sorry. You can't understand. I watch him looking for me, just sitting there in my room or down here, wasting all that time when he should be out with his friends, or getting ready for college, or . . . It's hurting him, and it's my fault. If I could go, if I wasn't here at all . . ."

She had no more control over that than Paige or the others did, of course. Though I couldn't help wondering if it might have something to do with her after all, something she didn't even realize. If her worries for Tim were holding her here, just like he couldn't let go of her. Of course, what dying person didn't have worries? But if she'd known just how messed up he'd be, between his dad taking off and his friends backing away . . . Maybe the pain on his face had been enough to make anyone want to stick around and watch over him.

I shook the thoughts away. I had no way of knowing, and it wouldn't change anything anyway.

"Could be once he talks to you he'll feel better about it," I suggested. "I can tell him he's only got five minutes. You listen for that long, and then we're all done, everyone goes back to their . . . lives."

"But . . . if he knows I'm here, it might be even harder for him to . . ."

"Move on?" I wanted to tell her there was no way, now that Tim was set on it, he wasn't letting go until he found her, but the hopelessness in her expression made me hesitate. There was only one thing I could say that might help. "If you want, I could tell him that I was wrong, that you're not here."

Her hands twisted together. "No," she said. "I never lied to him, and I don't want to start. Couldn't you just tell him I'm here? That I want him to start thinking about himself, instead of me?"

"I don't think that's going to do it for him," I said. "Seriously, if I could, I'd rather do it that way. But if you won't listen to him yourself, I think he's going to keep trying, and maybe that'll end up worse."

We watched each other for a long moment, and then she dropped her gaze.

"Okay," she said, quietly. "We'll try. Five minutes."

The front door creaked, and Tim stuck his head in. "Cass? What's going on?"

"I told you to wait," I said, glancing at his mom. She gazed past me to the door. After a second, she nodded.

"It's been forever," Tim was saying. "Have you even—"

"All right, all right." I sank down on the sofa. "Come in. She's here."

Tim stalked into the middle of the room, the door banging shut behind him. He swiveled on his feet, peering into the shadows. His mom hovered beside him. The light within her flickered.

"You're not going to be able to see her," I reminded him.

"Right." His mouth opened and closed and opened again.

"Over there." I tipped my head in her direction. "You should get going, whatever you wanted to say to her. We've got five minutes."

"Five minutes? Why?"

"She almost didn't stick around at all. She said you're thinking about her too much. It's bothering her."

"Thinking about her?" His forehead furrowed. "Mom?" he said. "Of course I'm thinking about you. Are you okay? I mean, it doesn't hurt anymore, does it?"

"No pain," she murmured, smiling.

"She says the pain's gone," I said.

"Good." He looked to me. "I'm sorry, it's not that I don't believe you, it's just . . . I need to know for sure that it's her."

I shrugged and raised my eyebrows at his mom. She slipped forward, just close enough to graze his shoulder with her fingers. Her gaze never left his face. "Before I went to the hospital the last time, I gave him my wedding ring to hold on to, so I knew it'd be safe."

"She says you've got her wedding ring."

His eyes widened. "She . . . she's really here." He spun around, as if he might catch a glimpse of her if he moved fast enough. "Okay. Okay. The ring . . . did you want me to give it to Dad? He hasn't asked about it, but I think he knows I have it."

"It's yours now. Do what you think is best."

"You can keep it. Or whatever you figure's best." I checked my watch. His time was half up, but maybe his mom would go easy on him, give him a little extra.

"Are you staying here?" Tim asked the shadows.

Her smile broke, falling to one side. "I don't know. I don't think it's my decision."

"She doesn't know. It doesn't seem to be up to them," I added. "As far as I can tell."

"Oh. I . . . Is there . . ." His voice faltered, and he stared at the floor. It occurred to me that he might have something to say that he didn't want me to hear, something between just him and his mom. Well, I couldn't help him there.

"I should go," his mom said.

"Hey, there's one more minute left," I told her. And then to Tim, "If there's anything else, you should say it fast."

"How can I . . . what should I do?" he blurted out, his voice so raw I glanced up from my watch. His face had gone pink and blotchy. "Everyone's . . . it's different now. People talk around me instead of to me, they act like it was nothing, like it was just an excuse to act sorry and make themselves feel good by pretending to care, like they don't even notice how I'm feeling. And Dad—I can't trust him. And Aunt Nancy's gone home, of course. There's no one. I don't know what to do."

His mom reached out, touching his cheek. "Tell him . . . tell him I've forgiven his father, and he should try to as well. Tell him he should live life the way he wants and stay close to people who care about him. There are people who care. And, please, he needs to look after himself. He's hardly sleeping. I think he's"—she shook her head. "I don't like it."

She kissed her fingers and brushed them over his forehead. "I'm here. I'm all right. Take care of you now." She drifted away into the wall.

I repeated her words to Tim. He didn't look up. After a minute of silence, I said, "She left. The room, I mean."

He sagged into the armchair in the corner, his shoulders slumping. I busied myself tugging at a thread in the sofa's upholstery. A thin, mildewy odor was starting to seep out of the cushions. Tim cleared his throat, but nothing came out.

We sat there in the dark, with the things he'd said, the things she'd said, things I'm sure he wished I hadn't heard, until I thought it all would smother me.

"I'll go," I said, standing up. "Should catch my P.M. classes."

Tim shifted to face me. The color had settled in his face and his eyes were clear, not teary. He pulled himself to his feet without much effort. But when he smiled, it looked like his face was going to crack across the middle and crumble away.

"Thanks," he said. "I mean, thanks doesn't say half of it, but I don't know what else to say."

"Don't worry about it," I said. "It's just something I can do, that's all." I hugged myself, my arms crossing my chest. I couldn't blame him if he was going to lose it for a bit, but I didn't think either of us wanted me to be there to see it. There was nothing I could say that would make it all right. I couldn't even comfort Paige about our mom, and I knew her better than anyone.

"Something no one else can do," he said, and laughed in a creaky sort of way. "So I guess I'll pick you up at nine tomorrow?"

Right. The party. I opened my mouth to protest, but something about the way he looked at me, that cracked smile, stopped those words from coming out.

"Okay," I said. "Nine it is."

CHAPTER 9

For Tim to be so flippant about cutting classes, I supposed the office was still going easy on him out of sympathy. Me, I missed four, and I got Mr. Gerry, the guidance counselor, breathing down my neck.

Mr. Gerry and I had been pals since my first day at Frazer. Mom and Dad thought, what with my freak-out over Paige's death and my miserable school performance thereafter, they ought to give the resident pseudoshrink a heads-up. So while everyone else was getting settled into first period, I had to sit on a saggy armchair and listen to this dorky little man tell me how my life was going to be. He had a face like an apple, all cheeks and a nub of a chin, with a mess of wiry curls on top. As he assured me that, if we worked together, my time at Frazer would be pleasant and productive, he smiled right across that apple face, trying to look like the most trustworthy guy in the universe.

"Don't be afraid to ask for help," he'd said, clamping his too big hands together over his knees. "That's what I'm here for."

He'd sure been "here" a lot. He'd hung around all through my freshman year, peeking into my classrooms and looking me over during lunch hour, fretting because I wasn't making any friends he could see, and I was making a whole lot of enemies. I'd get into a scuffle 'cause I'd told someone off, and he'd call me into his office. "Why do you try so hard to alienate your peers?" he'd whined, practically wringing his giant hands.

I don't know, I kind of wanted to say. Why had they tried so hard to alienate me? At least I only went after the ones who deserved it. But that didn't fit into Mr. Gerry's version of the universe, where everyone got along and everyone was happy.

After a while, of course, the kids had figured out it was safer to leave me alone than get in my face. And Norris had caught Mr. Gerry breaking school policy and a law or two in the teachers' underground parking lot. We'd come to an understanding. He still fretted over my absent friendships, but I wasn't getting into fights anymore, and I think he was starting to see that was as good as he was going to get.

That Friday, the day after my talk with Tim's mom, he must have been feeling especially dutiful. I'd slept in and had to hoof it to make it to school on time. It was five minutes before final bell, and the halls were packed. As the press of bodies dragged me past the guidance office, Mr. Gerry scampered out. With a couple of guys shouting about baseball rankings on my right and a bunch of girls gushing about some new romantic comedy on my left, I didn't hear him calling my name until he grasped my shoulder.

"Miss McKenna," he said. "A word?"

"What?" I squished myself around to face him. We were smack in the middle of the hall, holding up traffic.

Mr. Gerry made a pained expression. "In my office?"

"Class is about to start—"

He huffed into his cheeks, making them even rounder. "You will get a late slip. And if you refuse to speak with me, I will be obliged to call your parents and speak to them."

"I never said I wasn't coming," I said. Geez, you'd think the guy would appreciate my effort to get to class on time.

Mr. Gerry pushed back through the crowd, and I followed in his wake. The guidance secretary nodded at him as we squeezed out of the hall and into the reception room. Mr. Gerry opened his office door and waved me in.

There was a chair set in front of his desk, the same saggy one I'd sat in almost three years ago. I leaned against the filing cabinet instead. Mr. Gerry eyed his comfy wing chair. Sitting down, he could go into his favorite poses: bending forward with his chin on his hands, leaning back with his arms spread wide. If he did sit, though, he'd end up half my height. He opted to prop himself awkwardly against the paper-strewn desk.

"You've had several absences this week, Miss McKenna," he said. "You missed your afternoon classes on Wednesday and your morning classes yesterday. The office has not received a phone call from your parents, and you have not presented a note." Having laid out the facts, he paused to take a breath. "Could you tell me what's going on? Have you run into some trouble? Maybe there's something I could help you with."

I wondered if the office had already called Dad. If he'd

been absorbed in his work, he might have mumbled some excuse without even listening. Or maybe Mr. Gerry had held them off, so he could get a chance to talk to me first. Concerned about his own skin.

I just looked at him. He knew I ran into all sorts of trouble. I just usually attended classes in between. What did he expect me to say?

"Cassandra," he began.

"Cass," I said.

"Cass." He rubbed his nose and scratched at the back of his head. His curls jiggled. "Your grades are . . . passable. If you continue to miss classes, however, you may risk failing. You're an intelligent girl. I'm sure you can see this is a difficult situation."

"All right," I said. "I promise not to miss any more classes. Can I go?"

He paused with his hand on his neck. "I'm glad to hear that," he said. "If you're experiencing any . . . difficulties that you'd like to talk about, as your guidance counselor, of course I'm always here if you need me."

As if he'd really want to hear anything I had to say. Yeah, he was doing his job. But I knew my grades, and I hadn't been close to failing since that awkward period in ninth grade before I'd gotten my act sorted out.

"Mr. Gerry," I said, "I think I can handle this. I always have before, right? I don't get on your case about the stuff you snort at lunchtime, so how about you let me deal with this by myself?"

We looked at each other across the room for a good ten seconds. Then Mr. Gerry deflated onto his desk, his gaze skittering away. He reached up to rub his nose again, caught himself, and dropped his hand.

"The school year is almost over," he said. "Please try to keep your absences to a minimum."

"Not a problem, sir."

The bell rang as I stepped into the hall, but my first-period class was just upstairs. I hesitated for a second. Norris had been on Paul's car duty all yesterday afternoon and this morning. I was dying to know if he'd seen anything, but now didn't seem like the greatest time to tempt fate and Mr. Gerry's patience.

I plopped into my desk while Mrs. Waugh was taking attendance. Her eyes flickered toward me, but she said nothing.

In the ten-minute gap between classes, I dashed around the corner to my locker. Norris was floating by the ceiling, pacing in a slow circle. With his chin tucked in and his jacket collar pulled high, he looked like an overgrown vulture. A couple of kids were clanging around at their lockers, halfway down the hall. A bunch more were pouring out of the nearest classroom. I slipped by them and opened my locker.

"Hey, Norris."

He dropped down to my level, pushing his collar away from his face. A grin stretched his mouth from one end of his jaw to the other.

"You're not going to believe this," he said, eyes shining.

"What?" I said. "What happened?"

"Right. Okay." He coughed into his hand and cleared

his throat, as if he was getting ready for a presidential address. "So, I found Paul's car pretty quick yesterday. He parks it a block off Frazer Road. Nice set of wheels. Paul shows up with the girlfriend after school, lovey dovey, and they drive off. Not much going on. But this morning"—he rubbed his hands together—"I was cruising around the field 'cause you mentioned the track practice thing. And of course the team comes, runs around, Paul's there jogging across the field to warm up, and this girl wanders over and leans against the fence."

"The girl," I broke in, "was it Sharon? Kind of short and skinny, streaks in her hair, all different colors?"

"Yeah, that was her! Paul sees her, and goes kind of red, looking like he's afraid someone'll notice. He waves her off, and she goes, and I thought that was it. But then a couple minutes later, Paul's telling the coach he forgot a book in his car. So off he goes, and guess what—the girl's waiting for him when he gets there."

"Wow," I murmured. It had taken him, what, four days to pick up where he left off? Who knew how long they'd been messing around before this.

And Danielle hadn't had a clue. How could she not have seen?

She really trusted him, I thought, my throat tightening. She really thought he was crazy about her.

Just like I'd really thought we were friends. My jaw clenched, and I shook any sympathy I had away. The things she'd done, this was them coming back to haunt her. As it was only fair they should.

"And then?" I asked, prompting Norris.

"Right," he said. "So they meet up at the car, and Paul's telling her he can't be gone too long 'cause he doesn't want it to look suspicious, his girlfriend will get on his case, and Sharon says she can do something quick if he promises to see her that weekend. And, man, she was quick. I hardly blinked and down she went." Norris flushed. "I gotta say, if there's one thing I wish I hadn't missed, it's the things those girls can do."

"God," I said, "what a jerk. What an idiot! When I'd just caught him . . . God." Maybe he'd figured he was dead anyway, so he might as well make it worth it.

"That's not even the best part," Norris said. "Get this. While she was at it, her purse fell on the floor of the car, and a lipstick went rolling out, right under the passenger seat. Neither of them was paying attention, of course. Then she grabbed her stuff and went off who knows where, and he hurried on back to track practice, and no one noticed. So the thing's still there in the car."

My mouth dropped open, but I was so full of awe it took a couple of seconds to get the words out. "He screwed himself over. Totally."

"Oh, yeah."

"That's . . . thanks, Norris. You're the best. I wish I could stay to chat, but I've got to run to class. I'll come by at lunch, all right?"

"Excellent," he said as I grabbed my history binder from the locker. "Hey, you know that party you said you're going to tonight—who did you say was throwing it?"

"Matti Turuno. You know him."

"Yeah." Norris frowned. "I thought you'd want to

know, he was ranting to his girlfriend about something to do with that Tim guy, sounded really pissed. I only caught a bit of it, but I think I heard your name, too."

"Well, keep an eye on it, I guess." I closed my locker, my brain fizzing like pop that'd been shaken in the can. Of course. The party. I could topple Danielle and Paul like a couple of dominoes, and all their friends would be there to witness it. And I'd almost turned down the party invite. It was going to be a bash and a half.

Let Matti rant all he wanted. Nothing short of the Apocalypse could stop me now.

CHAPTER 10

When Paige first started going to parties, things were still all right between us. She'd drag me into her room, and I'd perch on the edge of her bed, chirping my approval of her hairstyle and dress choices on cue. Then I got old enough to want to borrow her clothes and makeup, and she decided I was too much of a nuisance. That didn't stop me from spying on her, of course. I'd peer through the keyhole or the gap at the edge of the door, or listen to her grumbles and sighs with my ear pressed close to the wall, until Mom found me and shooed me away. Even when I was so angry I wanted to strangle her with her pantyhose, curiosity was stronger.

Thanks to that, everything I know about party prep I learned from Paige:

1. Shower until the hot water runs out. Wrap hair in towel and scurry into bedroom.
2. Get the creamiest lotion you can find and rub it all over yourself.
3. Shimmy into a dress. Decide you look fat. Remove dress.

4. Pull on a skirt and blouse. Decide you look like a first-grader. Remove skirt and blouse.

5. Squeeze into the leather pants you've been hiding in the back of the closet. Decide it's too likely that Mom and Dad will pitch a fit at the sight of them. Stuff pants back into closet.

6. Throw on another dress. Check neckline (low enough?) and hemline (high enough?). Decide everyone will think you look like a cow, but you're too tired to try on anything else.

7. Mash gel into hair. Blow-dry upside down for volume.

8. Smother face with foundation, powder, eye shadow, blush, mascara, lipstick, and anything else you can dig out of the makeup drawer.

9. Spray perfume on bosom, neck, and hair.

10. Lounge on bed as motionless as possible, so as not to disturb the delicate balance of cosmetics, until your male attendant arrives.

I didn't bother with any of it except for number 1, because, really, people are a lot less likely to listen to you when you're grubby. I stepped into the same pair of jeans I'd worn to school and grabbed a T-shirt out of my closet at random. My hair I let air dry. Paige would've had a fit, but she'd conveniently wafted off sometime earlier, leaving nothing but a wisp of candied apples. She must have been missing Mom really bad if she was braving the airport to wait for the plane.

Looking at myself in the mirror, I decided there was

no way Tim's crowd could think I'd made any effort to look pretty for them.

Tim wasn't due for another twenty minutes. I went downstairs and flopped onto the couch next to Dad. He had Gilligan's Island on.

"What's the story?" I asked.

"The Skipper thinks he's onto some voodoo," Dad said, chuckling.

On the screen, Gilligan and the Skipper were arguing. My nerves crackled like fireworks. I tried to watch, but I kept losing track of what they were arguing about. After a few minutes, I squirmed down on the couch and lay my head on the armrest. The ceiling required less concentration.

The sound cut out as Dad muted the TV. "Cassie?" he said. I shifted so I could see his face.

"Yeah?"

Before he spoke, he took off his glasses, examined them, and slid them back on.

"This, ah, tonight, is this a date?"

I laughed. The chances of me having a date were less than none. It hadn't even occurred to me that it might look like one.

"Nah," I said. "I'll be hanging out with a bunch of people. The guy picking me up is just my ride."

"All right." He smiled, and I wondered if he was thinking about Paige running around with her date that last night. Maybe she'd jumped in the water only to impress Larry. Dads like to blame the boys.

I bet Paige would have gone for it whether there'd been a boyfriend around or not. She'd liked being a little crazy, trying it on for size. Dad had never known about the leather pants in the back of her closet. I'd snuck them out before he overhauled her room. They were in the back of my closet now.

"You'll be home by midnight?" Dad asked.

"Sure," I said. "If not before."

"Good, good."

"Don't worry, Dad. I'll look after myself."

I sat up and gave him a quick hug. Down the hall, the doorbell chimed.

"That must be your ride," Dad said. "Have a good time. And remember . . ."

"What?"

His smile turned sheepish. "To look after yourself."

"Of course." I squeezed his arm and jumped off the couch. As I reached the doorway, I had to force my feet to slow down. My skin was twitchy, and my heart was flip-flopping like a fish on a dock. It's just a party, I reminded myself. Just a bunch of kids hanging around. Nothing I couldn't handle. Sure, I hadn't been to one in more than four years, and a high school party was a far cry from pre-teen sleepovers—there would be lots of booze and no parents—and it was being held in the house of someone who hated my guts, but, really, what could go wrong?

I breathed slow and deep, exhaling the jitters as I walked along the front hall. Then I pushed my hair away from my face and opened the door.

"Hey." The porch light was off, and the shadows

softened the angles of Tim's face. His skin had more color than I remembered. Maybe the talk with his mom had helped, despite all her worrying. Good. I tried to give him a little smile, but I was so nervous my lips went crooked.

He tossed his keys from one hand to the other. "You ready to go?"

"Just a sec." I wiggled my feet into my boots, laced them up, and followed him out to the driveway. Tim wasn't much more dressed up than I was: polo shirt and khakis. If he saw anything wrong with my clothes, he didn't say so.

In the car, I leaned back and stretched out my legs as much as the cramped space allowed, watching the houses slip by. It was real now. I was going to this thing. My heart started jumping again. In just a few minutes, I could be face to face with Danielle. And Matti and Paul and a few dozen other people who'd sooner give me a kick in the head than the time of day.

Maybe this was a mistake. It was like going into enemy territory without a map. What if they ate me alive? There'd be enough of them there who'd want to.

I swallowed thickly. No. They wouldn't dare. No matter how many of them there were, no matter how many hated me, I had them scared. I had their secrets. They couldn't touch me.

Tim focused on the road ahead, where his headlights swam in the dusk. "I mentioned to Matti that you were coming with me," he said after a minute. "Since it is his party."

My mind leapt back to my conversation with Norris

that morning. So that was what Matti had been pissed off about. "He must have been overjoyed."

"He was pretty upset. Said I was crazy and stuff." Tim laughed sharply. "But I told him I'd already asked you to come, and I wasn't going back on that, and he let it go."

He sounded so determined about it I found myself saying, "You didn't have to. Not go back on it, I mean."

He glanced over at me. "You don't want to come?"

"Well—" It could easily be the best and the worst night of my life, rolled into one. But he was looking at me, he was talking, like it was important to him, and suddenly my heart was stuttering for a completely different reason.

Dad had asked—Tim couldn't think—he did know he was just my way into this thing, nothing more than that, didn't he?

"What about the rest of them?" I said quickly. "Do they all know?"

"Matti brought it up at lunch, so a lot of the Frazer people who'll be there know I'm bringing you. Does it matter?"

"No," I said. It didn't, did it? Danielle would still come, Paul would still come. They wouldn't want to admit that I made them nervous.

God, it was a good thing they didn't know how nervous I was.

Don't think like that. Stay focused. It's just a stupid party. Think of her face when you shove the truth in it. That's why you're here—because she deserves it.

Tim watched me for a moment longer before shifting

his gaze back to the road. I pretended not to notice. I couldn't think about him, or about anything except getting this thing done, not until it was over.

Matti's house beamed from the middle of its block, all the blinds up and the windows bright. It was a broad three-story, with a huge driveway that was already packed with cars. Tim pulled the Oldsmobile around in a U-turn and parked on the opposite side of the street. As I stepped out onto the sidewalk, he twisted around to grab a liquor bag from the back seat. Streams of music drifted out of the house. The beat was so faint that after a few seconds, I couldn't tell whether I was hearing anything more than my pulse thumping inside my head.

I picked out the cars under the streetlights: Jordana's yellow Bug, Flo's mom's tan Corolla, and Paul's Mustang, red as a ripe apple. Leon didn't drive to school, but he'd be there, by foot or in one of the cars I didn't recognize. Danielle would have come with Paul.

We crossed the street, Tim's bag clinking. I hung back as he rang the doorbell.

A guy I didn't know opened the door—he was from a different school, I guessed. "Cheers," he said, holding up a beer bottle. A sprig of chest hair showed where he'd left his shirt unbuttoned. His gaze dropped to Tim's bag. "Excellent, you brought the goods. Let's see what we've got."

He headed down the hall before we'd made it over the doorstep, and when Tim had pulled the door shut behind us, he loped after. Guitar chords crashed from the living room speakers, mixing with the movie voices warbling down the stairs from the second floor. Tim hadn't bothered taking off his shoes, so I left my boots on and edged along the wall to the living room.

Jordana and three other girls had wedged themselves onto the leather sofa. They chattered loudly to each other over the music. Jordana squealed with laughter. Leon stood in the corner, checking out the sound system as he sipped his drink. A couple of Frazer seniors were squatted on the floor with Matti's video game system, eyes glued to the TV. They punctuated every jab at their controllers with wordless shouts.

Jordana's gaze flickered my way briefly and then she went back to giggling with the other girls as if she hadn't seen me. Tim was in the kitchen, I figured, concocting a few drinks. Only a pathetic twerp would trail along at his ankles. He'd done me the favor of bringing me here; now I was on my own.

Past the sound system, I could see a corner of the dining room where cans of pop and bags of chips were scattered on a buffet. I crossed the room, my boots thudding on the hardwood floor, and swiped a root beer. Opening it, I settled back against the buffet.

A bunch of guys had an air hockey game set up on one end of the dining room table. "Hey, check this out," one of them said, tossing a beer cap onto the rink. It rattled back and forth a few times before flying off and landing on the floor. Matti poked his head in from the kitchen. He laughed with the guys and said something I couldn't hear. Then he saw me.

His mouth snapped shut, and he studied me for a moment, his eyes as narrow as the line of wispy hairs on his chin, where he was trying to grow a beard. He punched one of the air hockey guys in the shoulder, shouted something to another, and disappeared back into the kitchen.

As I craned my neck to check up on Jordana in the other room, Matti, Tim, and Mr. Chest Hair passed through the front hall and headed up the stairs. Tim glanced around and caught my eye, shooting me a quick smile. Matti elbowed him onward, scowling. Jordana waggled her fingers at him. When he'd passed out of sight with the others, she leaned over to look at a magazine her friends had opened.

Other than that one weird look from Matti, it was like I wasn't there. Maybe this was what it felt like being dead, unseen. As I scuffed my boots on the floor, a twitchy feeling crawled across my shoulders, making me squirm. I tried to gulp my root beer like I was perfectly content where I was. My hand shook. I set down the can.

Then Flo sauntered in. When she spotted me, she grinned and hustled over like we were best friends.

"Cass McKenna!" she said, her eyebrows arching, her smile baring all her teeth. "I heard you were coming, but I didn't believe it until now. Enjoying our scene?"

Good old Flo. Maybe it was time she found out what it was like to have someone shove their nose into her business.

"It's all right," I said.

"I always thought, 'That Cass, she'd be a good girl to get to know.' Bet you've got all kinds of great stories. You ever think of writing them down?"

Big surprise—she was mining me for newspaper

material. Funny how she was so eager to talk to me now, when she'd never said a word to me in the nearly three years we'd gone to school together. I might have been flattered if I hadn't known she was just softening me up so she could drag whatever information she wanted out of me.

I shrugged. "I'm not sure the teachers would appreciate the sort of articles I'd write."

"Aw, I'd find a way to swing it past them. Maybe tackle more general topics instead of specific people, but there's still a lot of meat in that." Flo waved her hand dramatically. "Can you imagine? We'd be the coolest student paper ever, with the kind of exposés you specialize in. Nothing like the brutal truth to shake things up."

Now that she'd relaxed, her smile was more friendly than predatory. Maybe she meant it, after all. I eyed her. "You'd really want me to write for the *Gazette*?"

"Of course," she said. "Heck, I'd have come after you sooner, but . . . you're not exactly approachable, you know? But you're here, so I figured, best chance I'm going to get."

I was speechless. This honesty didn't fit with the girl I'd expected, given what I knew.

She seemed to take my silence as indecision. "Well, think about it, okay? You want to talk, I'm sure you know where to find me at school."

Grabbing a handful of ketchup chips, she headed over to make eyes at Leon. I let out a breath and picked up my root beer.

Well, that hadn't gone exactly the way I'd expected. Had someone slipped a niceness pill in her drink?

The air hockey guys were shooting me strange looks. I guessed it wasn't cool to spend the whole evening staked out by the snacks. Time to move on, then.

As I left the buffet, Danielle came sashaying into the living room. She flopped into a tiny space that opened on the sofa beside Jordana. She'd gotten dressed up for the party, of course: a flared dress with an empire waist in the same cut-grass green as her eyes, and a flowery faux-gold choker. Her hair was pumped up with mousse, her feet bare, each perfect toenail painted coral pink. Paige would have approved.

My stomach turned, and I looked away. I wasn't ready for her yet. My fingers tightened around the can, and I hurried past the air hockey players to the kitchen.

A couple of Frazer juniors were fishing pizza out of boxes on the counter, and a couple more were pawing through the bottles in the fridge. The pearl-gray room smelled like grease and fried cheese. My boot squelched in a puddle of soda. I squeezed over to the sink and stared into it, like I was looking for something.

Of course she's here, I told myself. You knew she'd be here. That was the point. Get it together.

"There are clean glasses in the dishwasher." Matti cocked his head toward the speckled appliance at my right, aiming a glare at me. The juniors scuttled away from the fridge, and he leaned into it, grabbing a bottle, his eyes never leaving me. With the dark locks and the smooth baby face, I'm sure he'd have looked like a real sweetheart if it hadn't been for the scraggly pseudobeard and the daggers in his eyes.

He probably meant it to intimidate me, but instead I felt steadied. Hostility I could deal with.

"You want a drink?" he asked, like he was offering me a knuckle sandwich.

"Got one," I said, raising my can. "Thanks anyway."

He closed the fridge and set down the bottle, unopened. His hand clenched against the counter. "Look," he said, "I don't know what you think you're doing here—"

"Maybe you should ask Tim," I suggested. "It was his idea."

"Yeah, sure, and monkeys will fly out of my butt."

"That'll be interesting to see."

He glowered at me. "The point is, this isn't school. This is my house. I bet you have all your little secrets ready to throw in everyone's faces—well, no one cares here. You even look at anyone funny and I'll kick you out so fast you'll think you never left home."

I couldn't blame Matti for being grouchy. Back when I'd first gotten started at Frazer, he and a couple of friends had been making a buck a pop selling cheat copies of the winter exams to freshmen. The worst thing was, Norris overheard them snickering about how they'd pulled one over on the new kids. The exam copies weren't real— they'd made up the questions themselves. The kids were paying for the privilege of failing.

Back then, I hadn't learned yet that it was better for me and more humiliating for them if I kept student business between students. The teachers got involved, parents got called, and some people ended up temporarily suspended.

Yeah, I'd been stupid. But Matti was more stupid if he figured he could get burned only once.

"Kick me out?" I flicked at a stray chip. "So that'd be like how you got Paul kicked off the list for athlete of the year? Funny about that, 'cause he still seems to think you're his best bud."

Matti's face twitched and his mouth tightened. He held my gaze, scowling.

"Hey," I said, "I'm still here."

"You're not going to tell him."

"Try to push me out the door and we'll see if I do. It's got to happen sometime."

He looked down, popped the cap off the bottle, and took a long swig. After a few gulps, he smacked it down on the counter.

"You know what's pathetic?"

"I have the feeling you're going to tell me," I said, bracing myself.

"What's pathetic," he said, "is a reject like you trying to blackmail some guy into being your boyfriend."

I stared at him. "What are you talking about?"

"Oh, come on. That's got to be it. You found some nasty thing on Tim, and you're working it as hard as you can. Or maybe you've cast a little spell on him. Whatever it is, it's pathetic."

Clearly, he was not only a jerk, but also completely insane.

"What would I want Tim for?" I said. "I didn't even—He came after me."

"Yeah, yeah, and he won't dare deny that." He

pointed the mouth of the bottle at me, sneering. "You pretend you're so high and mighty, but you're the worst of any of us."

"Hold on. I don't want anything to do with Tim. I'll probably never even talk to him again after tonight."

"Good. You'd better. If you don't leave him alone, then—"

I folded my arms over my chest. "What if he doesn't leave me alone?"

"Not going to happen. There's no way." Matti shook his head. "And if you don't back off, then someone will have to do something about it."

He plucked a cigarette out of his shirt pocket and stalked off toward the back door. In the living room, the music petered out as the playlist ended. Voices dropped and halted in the sudden quiet.

My mouth was paper-towel dry. I drained the last of my root beer, but it just made my throat feel sticky.

I'd been an idiot. Of course they assumed I was manipulating Tim. Forget that all I'd ever done was throw out the truth for people to deal with it—that I'd never forced anyone to do anything, except maybe face facts. There just wasn't enough room in their tiny brains for the idea that Tim might want anything to do with me. And even Dad had asked me if this was a date. Wonderful. I looked like every other ditz at school, scrambling to get my paws all over Mr. VP. They thought I'd made him bring me to the party— what else did they figure we'd been doing? I cringed.

Squaring my shoulders, I tossed my can in the sink. They could think what they wanted. It wasn't like I could change their minds without getting into some long explanation of the dead and all, which they wouldn't believe anyway. But I could make Matti regret threatening me. I'd been holding on to that dirt for the right moment, when Paul was most likely to listen, but if Matti wanted to push it out of me now, let him push.

I strode into the front hall. Where was Paul? He had to be around here somewhere. A carload of girls had just arrived, prancing through the door, tossing their hair like a bunch of show horses, and I backed into the living room to let them pass. As I cocked my head toward the stairs to listen for Paul's voice, a hand tapped my shoulder.

"What?" I said, twisting around. The first thing I saw was a ripple of bronze hair. My heart plummeted.

"I need to talk to you," Danielle said. Her voice was quiet, but I could hear the edge in it. I turned to face her, my pulse skittering.

Fine. If she wanted a piece of me right now, let her come and try to take it.

"So talk," I said.

She rolled her eyes and gestured to a door by the stairs. "Not here. Come—"

"I'm not going anywhere," I said. Like I was going to let her haul me off somewhere to bitch at me—if she wanted to be nasty, she could do it where all her friends could see. "If you want to talk, talk now."

She glanced around. Everyone else was too involved in their own conversations to pay much attention to us. Crossing her arms over the ruched bodice of her dress, she shifted closer to the wall. I followed her.

"All right," she said. "But I don't want to hear all your stupid comments that don't mean anything. Let's get to the real deal. What do you know?"

I caught myself just short of gaping at her. She was *asking* me to spill everything I knew? Here, surrounded by all the people she'd dressed to impress? Since when did she even believe I had anything real to tell?

She must have read the confusion on my face. "You're obviously here for a reason," she said. "After Paul heard you were coming, he suddenly thought maybe there were more interesting things we could be doing. So I want to know what's going on."

Just like Danielle. Knowing it was going to come, determined to make it go her way, not mine. I wasn't going to make it that easy for her.

I lowered my head, examining my fingernails. "What part do you want to know? What happened Monday, or what happened today?"

Danielle hesitated. In the same moment, Paul stepped into the living room, gesturing toward Leon. He saw us and froze. The color washed out of his face. Then he started across the living room toward us.

"Dani, we talked about it. She's just—"

"Shut it, Paul," Danielle snapped. "I'm asking Cassie."

Paul halted, stricken. Gunshots rang out from the TV upstairs. The beer bottles were clinking in the dining room, the chip bags crinkling, the fridge gasping open and thudding closed. But the girls on the sofa, the guys with their game controllers, the newcomers jostling through the hall, they all lowered their voices, watching.

I looked at Danielle. She'd wanted to do this all quiet and secretive, but there wasn't a chance of that now. I waited for her to make some excuse and slip away, but she set her jaw and shrugged.

This was my moment. I should have been trembling with joy, but all I felt was a cold shiver that rippled right down to my gut. Maybe it was because of the messed-up situation with Tim; maybe it was the kindness Flo had offered; I didn't know. But suddenly doing it like this, in front of everyone, didn't seem like justice. It just seemed horrible.

I turned away from her, from them, and walked to the door Danielle had motioned to before. It opened into a small den—computer desk, bookshelves, silence.

Danielle came in behind me, frowning. "Look," she said, tugging the door shut, "I'm sick of the hints and insinuations. Just spit it out. All of it."

Remember seventh grade, I told myself. Remember that first time she turned away.

I dragged in a breath, and my mouth formed a hard little smile.

"Well," I said, "I'm missing some important details, like why you think your boyfriend's such a catch when he spends most of his time being a prick, but basically . . . Monday morning he was groping Sharon Lietzer in the equipment shed after track practice. And this morning he invited her into his car, and she, um, provided some action below the belt."

Splotches of color rose in Danielle's cheeks. "If you're making this up . . . ," she said, her voice shaking.

I looked her straight in the eyes. "I wouldn't do that," I said. "That's not how I work, unlike some people. And if you're worried about it, you can always check under the passenger seat. Sharon left her lipstick behind."

As the words spilled from my mouth, the door jerked open. Paul stared in at us. If the pallor of his face was anything to go by, he'd heard enough to know he was screwed.

"I, uh, I guess you're still busy," he said, starting to back away.

"Paul," Danielle said, "stay right there or I'll dump you without even looking."

"Just . . . just didn't want to interrupt," he muttered, going still. Danielle pointed her long, manicured finger-nail at me.

"You love this, don't you, Cassie? You get to take your jabs at everyone and gloat about it, and wow, that must be so much fun."

"No, I—" I hate it, I almost said. I hate that you can't all just own up to what you've done. I hate that if I don't do something about it, no one will. At that moment, I even hated the pain on her face, I hated that Paul had thought it better to fool around on her instead of just breaking up, I hated that I had been the one to tell her. It was all a sickening lurch in my stomach and a hollow ache in my chest.

"You're all so full of crap—you expect no one to notice?" I said. "One person stands up to you, and—"

Danielle tossed her hair. "Please, spare me. You're just mad at me. I don't like you much, either, so that's okay.

But don't try and pretend this isn't your stupid 'revenge' for stuff that happened a million years ago. We're in high school now. Grow up and get over it."

She stepped out of the den and jabbed her hand toward the front door. "Let's go, Paul. Sharon'll want her lipstick back."

Paul shuffled around looking fierce, but as soon as Danielle reached the door he bolted after her. Their voices drifted in, muted, from outside: "Babe, Dani, it wasn't that big a thing." and Danielle's bark of a laugh. Leon had started the music going again in the living room, and the babble of gossip flowed over the music.

I slipped out into the hall and sagged against the wall, feeling it solid and smooth against my side. It was done. I'd slain her. So where was the joy? Where was the release? My mouth burned like I'd just thrown up. I inhaled the smell of onion rings and almost gagged.

Tim emerged from the cluster of kids at the base of the stairs. I peered up at him without raising my head.

If Tim knew what had happened, or cared, it didn't show. He glanced toward the door and made the pained smile I'd always hated. For once, it seemed to fit.

"There you are," he said, and cocked his head. "Time to go?"

I'd just ripped up three of his best friends. In a world that made sense, he'd be telling me to walk. But I wasn't up to arguing.

"Yeah," I said. "Let's get out of here."

CHAPTER
11

Night had crept over the city while we were inside. The street got even darker as we walked away from the glow of the house. Paul's Mustang was gone, leaving an empty rectangle on the cobblestone driveway. Danielle must have decided they'd put on a big enough show already. Tim's Oldsmobile stood under a streetlamp, shimmering its brilliant baby blue. I let Tim hold open the door for me.

The cool air followed me in, and the leather seat welcomed me. How many times had I sat there in the last week? I was too wiped to count. Right now it was nice just to feel something familiar. Resting the side of my head against the back of the seat, I gazed out the window. Beyond the circle of lamplight, the world was solid black. Like it was just me and Tim and the clunky old car.

Tim started the ignition. The engine hiccuped a few times and settled into a steady hum. He rested his hand on the gearshift, still in park.

"Someone said you and Danielle were friends?" he asked. In the shadows of the car, his eyes were only gray. "She never mentioned it."

"It's not something she likes people to know."

"I take it that it ended badly."

I shrugged. In the house, they'd be able to look out the living room windows and see us sitting there.

"Can we just go?"

"Okay, no problem."

He sounded offended. How could he not care what they were saying? It should have bothered him more than it did me. Maybe he didn't realize just what they were saying now.

As he pulled onto the road, I wiggled down farther in the seat and propped my knees against the dashboard. To anyone outside, it'd look like I wasn't even there. Maybe if I closed my eyes, I wouldn't be.

"So you're just not going to tell me," Tim said, abruptly. "I'll have to ask Danielle."

My eyes flicked open, and I glanced at him. His expression was blank.

"Whatever you want," I said.

"Fine. I'll believe whatever she says, then."

What was this, second grade? "If you think that's a good way to get me to spill my guts," I said mildly, "you must think I'm an idiot."

"I don't think you're an idiot." Tim exhaled sharply. "Don't you realize that you're a really hard person to talk to? I'm just trying to find a way that works, okay?"

"Well, baiting me isn't the way to go."

"What if I said I want to understand, you know, why this is important to you?"

"Because it's a fascinating story?" I snorted.

"Okay, so look at it this way, then. If someone I hang

out with, like Danielle, has done something so bad you'd want to get revenge on her . . . well, I'd like to know about it. I mean, should I be watching my back?" His lips crooked. "Maybe she's a murderer or a perpetual liar or a kleptomaniac. How'm I supposed to know, if you won't talk about it?"

"There," I said. "At least that's a reason that makes sense. All right."

I thought I'd rattle off the facts fast and snappy, pare the situation down to the cold hard bones, leaving out the fat and the gristle. But as I opened my mouth, emotion welled in my throat, and I couldn't speak. It was too much to squeeze into one easily digestible mouthful. I had to take a step back.

"We started hanging out in third grade," I said, staring into the dark space beyond the windshield. "That was when her dad got transferred here from Chicago. We hit it off, you know, like kids do. My mom used to say she couldn't have pried us apart with a crowbar. We were *best* friends, if you can believe it. Until junior high. In junior high there was Jordana and this other girl who ended up going to Mountview instead of Frazer—Sloane—and we all called each other best friends."

That was how junior high worked. You clustered. One cluster might get along with another sometimes, depending on moods and feuds, but you were guaranteed your one group of three or four or five friends, for hanging out in the halls, for sharing lunches, for cruising the mall after school.

The whole time, though, I'd kept thinking of Danielle

as my real best friend. We had the extra four years between us, that back history of friendship bracelets and sleepovers and secret sharing. Jordana spent too much time flicking her skirt at the boys, and Sloane had nothing in her head until you put an idea there. Danielle was the one who got things going, who decided which halls we'd hang out in and which shops we'd cruise. Yeah, she was bossy sometimes. It bugged her that Mr. Hesse gave me more solo parts in choir, so I switched to band. No big deal. We were friends; you just did that stuff. And she was always fun to be around. She had a sixth sense for where the action was going to be, and if there wasn't anything happening, she'd get something started.

It had never occurred to me that someday she'd feel the need to start something against me.

"So then what?" Tim asked. "You had a fight?"

"No. It wasn't like that. It's . . . hard to explain."

A fight would have been better. If she'd thrown it in my face, accused me, insulted me, I could have argued, I could have explained. But then she'd have looked like a jerk. So she waged her war against me in whispers and passed notes, nasty phrases written on chalkboards, glares shot from across the room. And she waged it with an army. Within a week, it seemed like every girl in school giggled as they "accidentally" trod on my toes or bumped into me from behind. It didn't take long before the boys were in on it, too, scrawling obscenities on my desk and kicking around the books they knocked out of my arms. Everyone else was doing it, why not join in? I started walking close to the walls and sitting in the back corners of the classrooms. And if I walked up to Danielle, all I got was her back. There was nothing to fight.

"It sounds silly," I said. "We were on debate team together—that was a big thing at school, and there was a guy on the team Danielle liked. The teacher in charge picked me to go to state finals, with that guy. I didn't even know until it was on the announcements. But Danielle must have figured I'd hid it from her, maybe even convinced Mr. Bridges to choose me instead of her . . . I don't know. Everyone was making a big deal about it, congratulating me, and then the guy asked me to go out for burgers to celebrate when she was standing right there—"

"It bugged her that you were getting all that attention."

My back felt stiff. I squirmed upright in the seat. "I don't know exactly what went on in her head. She stopped talking to me. I told Mr. Bridges I couldn't do state, and I turned down the guy, but it was too late. She'd already made up her mind. And she never did things halfway."

Tim turned the wheel, hand over hand, and stopped with a smoothness that surprised me so much it took a few seconds before I realized we were in my driveway. Dad had left the porch light on. It painted yellow stripes through the railing onto the lawn. The windows were dark. I wondered if he was lying inside there half awake, waiting for that click of the door before he could drift all the way into sleep, the way I'd used to wait for Paige.

"And everyone just went along with her?" Tim said. He twisted sideways in his seat, pulling up one of his legs so the ankle crossed the opposite knee. Getting comfortable, like he thought we were going to be here for a while. My scalp prickled. Why was he so interested, anyway? Did I want him to know all this?

"People liked Danielle," I said quickly. "She chatted everyone up, she smiled with lots of teeth. You know." I hesitated. "It didn't help that a month later I was seeing dead people in the halls and freaking out about my sister. No one needed convincing that there was something wrong with me after that. Anyway, there's always someone getting picked on, isn't there? So when someone gets chosen, and it isn't you . . . who's going to stand up to be the new target? It's not like every single person was harassing me, but anyone who wasn't . . . they just stayed out of it, stayed away."

Tim nodded. "Girls are strange that way. With guys, you just punch each other until someone backs down, and the next day it's done."

"Depends. I've seen the guys at Frazer pull just as much crap as the girls do. Everyone pulls crap." I looked at my hands, my fingers twisting together on my lap. "I'm surprised you haven't noticed. Your friends are full of it."

Tim's gaze fell. He grimaced at the gearshift, scratching the back of his neck.

"Yeah, well," he said, "I've been noticing a lot more since Mom died. They're jerks a lot of the time. I know. You know, they hardly came by my place after she got sick. It's like I can't even talk to them about her. They just get that look on their faces, and I can tell—they don't want to deal, they don't want to hear it. They don't even care that . . ." He swallowed thickly. "I just don't know what to do about it. Maybe it's a good thing there's someone like you putting them in their places now and then."

"Somehow I don't think they'd agree with you."

"Well, screw them, then." He paused. "It's weird. I guess I just assumed they were good friends. We hung out, we talked about stuff that I guess didn't really matter, they were there when it was easy. But now it's gotten so obvious something's missing. . . ."

As if his friends had ever been great people. He'd just decided not to see what they were like until it was him getting the cold shoulder.

"Hey," I said, "you're the one who keeps hanging out with them. And since we're on the subject, Matti's creeping me out. Maybe you could tell him next time you talk to him that I'm not trying to steal your soul or something."

"Yeah," Tim said. "He was getting on my case at the party. I'll say something to him. I mean, hell, why shouldn't I talk to you? You're the only one who actually says what you're thinking, not just what you figure won't be too uncomfortable. No one else has asked me anything about her, or what happened—not just how I'm doing and here's some pretend sympathy and now let's change the subject." He smiled. "I appreciate that, you know."

The car, suddenly, felt way too small. "I, uh, you're welcome, I guess," I mumbled. "Well, we're here—"

"Wait." He reached around to the back seat, where his backpack sagged on the floor, and dug through one of the pockets. "You're going to think this is really dumb," he said, "I know. But the committee's just about given up on selling the rest so they gave freebies to everyone on the student council, and, I mean, everyone else I know already has one, and, well—here."

He handed me a rectangle of printed cardstock. I looked down at it and almost bit my tongue.

The paper was lightly textured, with slanted black lettering on a creamy background. The Sixty-fourth Annual Frazer Prom. Just like Paige's, except hers had been the sixtieth. I guess they got the prom tickets printed at the same place every year.

Tim was hovering somewhere at the edges of my vision. I couldn't quite bring myself to raise my eyes.

"You want me to go to prom," I said, trying to make it seem like a laugh. It sounded more like I was choking on something.

"I just—I had the extra tickets—I mean, why not, right? You don't have to go. I don't even know for sure that I'm going. But, if I do . . . it wouldn't be such a bad thing for there to be someone else there who isn't a total jerk, right?"

What do you know, I wanted to ask him, about who's a jerk and who's not? Something had tightened up inside of me. It didn't feel right—he shouldn't be giving me things like this, saying things like that—I shouldn't be taking. I didn't have the right. What had I done, except what he'd badgered me into doing, because I thought I could get something for myself out of it? Maybe his old friends weren't so great, but I wasn't his friend either. I didn't even know how to be. I hardly knew how to be friends with people who'd been dead for decades.

"Well, thanks," I said. "For . . . this, and the ride. I should go in."

"Are you okay?" He peered at me, his eyes rounding in concern.

"I'm fine." My hand slipped on the door handle. I grasped it and pushed. The door popped open and I teetered out into the dewy air. I'd been tired when I left Matti's. Now I was exhausted.

"Have a nice drive," I said, and shut the door. The middle step creaked as I scrambled up to the porch, feeling for my keys in my pocket. The Oldsmobile was silent. I jerked the house key in the lock and burst into the hall, shoving the door shut behind me. My heart thudding, I leaned back against it. After a moment, I heard the squeak of tires on asphalt and the rumble of the engine fading away.

Upstairs, I realized I still had the prom ticket clutched in my hand. I dropped it into a desk drawer and shoved it out of sight. Peeling off my clothes in the dark, I groped along the bed for my pajamas. The whole house was quiet, a vacuum left by Paige's absence. My brain started filling in its own noise: Matti's threats, Danielle's laugh, Tim's last words. *Are you okay?* My eyes started to burn. I burrowed into the bed and hugged my pillow. When I was asleep, it'd be gone, all of it.

The air overhead shivered. A glow fell across my face. "Cassie?" Paige's voice called out.

"What?" I murmured into the pillow, hoping she'd mistake it for a snore and leave me alone, this once.

"Where've you been?" she asked, dipping over me.

The glow on my eyelids shone brighter. "I started feeling icky at the airport so I came home, and you weren't here, and then Dad went to bed, and everything was dark. . . . I went out looking for you. I was worried."

I flipped onto my back and opened my eyes. Paige shimmered over the foot of the bed, her ghostly knees pulled up to her chest and her arms wrapped around them. She stared at me, unblinking.

"I went out," I said. All my words, it seemed, had dried up. "To a thing."

"What kind of a thing?"

"A bunch of poseurs hanging out together kind of thing. Don't worry. I'm fine." As fine as a person could be after telling her life story to a guy she'd never have given the time of day to a week ago. Oh, and then having a panic attack over a prom ticket. Yes, I was fine.

Paige ducked her head behind her knees. Her hair drifted over her face. "I know," she said, her voice petulant and embarrassed at the same time. "It's just you're always here. How was I supposed to know what was going on? You could have been anywhere. Anyway, there's nothing to do when you're gone."

I yawned. "I'd have told you about it if you'd been here after school."

"I was waiting for Mom. The calendar said her plane was coming at five, but I never saw her." She sighed. "Airports are confusing."

"It's just a delay," I said. "There's always a delay. She'll get here."

She just wouldn't stay.

"She was away a long time, this time. At least, it seemed like it . . ." Paige trailed off, confused by her scrambled memories.

"I know," I said. "Dad said she'll be here the whole weekend."

"Oh, good." Paige smiled. "It's nice to see her, even though . . ." The smile faltered.

"I know," I said again. There was nothing I could do about that. My mind started to drift away. Paige glided along the bed, dimming to a faint shimmer. She hovered over me until my eyes slid closed, and then she whispered, timidly, "Cassie?"

I blinked. "What?"

"I just thought . . ." She hesitated, and I could almost hear her breathing beside me, except she didn't breathe anymore. "You remember how we used to have pajama parties? Stay up real late, eat popcorn, watch old movies on TV? Do you think we could do that again sometime? It was so much fun."

Sure, I remembered. In particular, I remembered the last time, when I'd been eleven and she fifteen, and I'd had to beg her to sit with me through one movie. She'd made such a production of sighing impatiently and painting her nails during the best parts that I'd never asked her again.

But now she was asking me.

I pulled myself upright and felt on my desk for the remote. The TV came on blaring. I fumbled with the volume control before switching to the channel listings station. Funny, this was the TV we'd always used before.

I'd never had one of my own until Dad cleaned out Paige's room and handed hers over to me.

"This'll be great!" Paige stretched out on the bed against the wall. I scooted over a couple of inches, as if she needed the space. "I guess there's no point in making popcorn," she said.

"It always made the sheets greasy, anyway." I watched the channel guide slide upward. "There's a Katharine Hepburn movie that just started."

"Oooh, let's watch that one."

I jogged through the channels to the movie, then sank down so my head rested against the pillow. Paige squirmed beside me like a five-year-old on Christmas Eve. After that mess of a party, it was a small relief to know this, at least, I could do right. She giggled as the actress shot off a clever line of dialogue, and her pale hand groped for mine, passing through it with a tingle. My eyes felt so heavy I knew I wasn't going to make it through the movie. Paige wouldn't mind.

Strains of violin swayed out of the speakers. My eyelids drooped. For a moment, Paige was just a smattering of light between my lashes, and then I was asleep.

CHAPTER 12

Of all the awful things I could wake up to on any given morning, the worst had to be my mom's voice, when she had that tone like I'd managed to screw up the universe without even being conscious.

"Cassie. Cassie!" she was saying. I opened one eye and peered at her through my hair. She was standing in my bedroom doorway with her suitcase at her feet, her lips pressed in a glossy line and her auburn bob neat and sleek. Either she primped in the taxi or she'd secretly mastered the art of teleportation. I guessed she figured if she was perfect when she was here, it'd compensate for all the times she wasn't.

She knocked the door frame, her knuckles rattling against the wood. That sound made my bones shudder. I yawned and propped myself up on my elbow.

"Hi, Mom."

She crossed her tanned arms and raised her eyebrows. "How many times have I reminded you about turning off the TV before you go to sleep? You know my editor's been cutting his freelance people. The last thing I need to worry about is the electricity bill."

Well, hello and good morning to you, too. I hauled myself over the pillow and grabbed the remote. The pastel colors of a Saturday morning cartoon flickered to black. If Mom was in any danger of losing her job, I doubted the magazine would be paying for her to jet around the world every other week, but it was easier not to argue.

"You just got in?" I asked. The clock said seven.

"They ended up canceling my flight—mechanical difficulties. I had to wait for the red-eye. I called your father to let him know."

"Dad was in bed when I got home," I said, rubbing the sleep from my eyes. Mom's eyebrows leapt up twice as high as before.

"It was nothing"—I jumped in before she could start a barrage of questions. "I just met up with a few people from school, drank a root beer."

"Well, I'm glad to hear you're finally attempting to develop a social life." She picked up her suitcase. "You look tired. Get some more sleep."

If she hadn't suggested it, I might have zonked right out, but the second the words came out of her mouth, I started feeling edgy. It wasn't so bad when she was home during the week and I was in school most of the day, but a whole weekend of nothing but Mom . . . just enough time for her to go all hyper-maternal on me and satisfy her guilt before she packed up again.

I flopped back on the bed and stretched my arms up over my head. Paige had disappeared. I bet she was in Mom and Dad's bedroom, eager to hear Mom dish about the trip. The food was all right but the atmosphere dull. The hotel service was friendly, but the in-house entertainment lacked pizzazz. Or the other way around. Even when Mom got sent to interesting places, like the Mardi Gras celebrations or the Olympics, by the time she got home she didn't have much more to say besides how loud the people were, how crowded the streets, how hectic her schedule. Any enthusiasm she had left, she poured into her articles.

I lay there until I was sure I couldn't fall back asleep, and then I crept downstairs to make breakfast. If I hurried, I could eat before Mom came down and started lecturing me about proper nutrition. I didn't see why she bought bacon if she didn't want me eating it.

As the fat hissed in the frying pan, I dropped a slice of bread into the toaster and reconsidered last night's events. It hadn't gone that badly, really. I'd given the opportunity my best. So what if no great weight had lifted off my shoulders now that I'd had it out with Danielle—I'd been silly to think it would. I'd live, like I always had.

Mom came down as I was finishing up my toast. The stairs creaked, and I shoved the last bit of crust into my mouth, jumping up to stick my plate in the dishwasher. Not quite fast enough. I turned around, and there she was in the doorway. Great. Inquisition time.

"I'm going to make some tea," she said, smoothing her hair back. She'd changed from her posh skirt and blazer to a linen dress, and her bob was slightly rumpled. "Do you want any? You could try the one that's supposed to be good for your complexion."

And here I thought my skin had been looking all right

lately. I touched my cheek. "Um, no thanks. I was going to get started on my homework."

"You've got all weekend for that. Stay awhile. I want to hear all about what you were up to last night." She brushed past me, plucking the kettle from the counter and dipping it under the tap.

Mom didn't get that there were several valid reasons for me not to tell her about last night, for her own good. For starters:

1. The very thought of a boy inviting me to a party would cause such an explosion of joy that she'd have a heart attack.
2. Even in the middle of said heart attack, she'd have to ask me all sorts of embarrassing questions, like whether the boy and I were "seeing each other," when we were "going out" again, and whether I'd gotten a good-night kiss.
3. The answers to those questions ("Ha!" "I'd guess around the time Hell freezes over," and "No, thank God!") would throw her into such despair that her heart would kick right out and she'd die on the spot.

In a way, it was Paige's fault. No way could I live up to Miss Popularity herself. I'm sure it looked obvious to Mom—Paige happy, Cassie not so happy; Paige social butterfly, Cassie social misfit; therefore, social butterfly equals happy. As if that was the only difference between me and her. For one thing, Paige hadn't had a dead sibling living in her bedroom.

I couldn't leave now without starting a scene, which would have been worse in the long run. So I improvised.

"It was for class, really," I said. "We have to do group presentations for, um, geography class. The six of us got together in the evening to work on it, ordered some pizza, that's about it."

"Sounds like it wasn't all work, then. Might have been a good opportunity to make friends. I hope you made a little effort."

I have friends, I wanted to tell her. You just wouldn't believe they exist.

She bent over to shuffle through the tea drawer for the Earl Grey. "If you need to meet up again, you should invite them over here. People appreciate that sort of gesture."

"We're just about finished," I said. "The last part we're supposed to do in class anyway."

"Well, if you ever want to invite someone over just for fun—"

"I know, Mom." What did she think this was—preschool? Actually, she'd probably like that. She could call the other parents and arrange visits and schedule friends into my life, without even having to talk to me about it.

"I was thinking," she said, "maybe you're not meeting people who have enough in common with you. There's always lots going on at that rec center on Granmore. We could sign you up for a club, or some sort of classes."

"I don't know," I said. "I'll take a look." I couldn't think of anything I'd want to take classes in. The art of death management?

The kettle started to whistle, and while Mom was distracted, I slipped out of the kitchen. Grabbing a couple of graphic novels I hadn't gotten around to reading yet, I curled up in a chair on the back patio. With a little luck, it wouldn't occur to her to look for me there until I'd already left to catch that movie with Norris.

Other than a little poking about the classes idea at dinner and a couple questions about the movie (well, Norris loved it), Mom let me be for the rest of Saturday. By Sunday morning, it was starting to seem like I would get through the entire weekend without a full-blown lecture. I wondered if Dad was actually right this time. Maybe she was trying to ease off.

Then the phone rang.

Mom picked it up, her bright and perky voice carrying up the stairs.

"Hello? Oh, yes, just a second. I'll get her."

Her footsteps padded up, and she peeked into my room. "Cassie," she whispered, as if the caller might hear us, "there's a boy on the phone for you."

Here was a moment for the history books: My first call from a member of the opposite sex. No doubt she'd bronze the phone in memory of the occasion.

"Okay," I said, giving her my best bored voice so she'd know this wasn't a potential boyfriend or something, and reached for my phone. Mom flitted off to share the excitement with Dad.

I was too busy being annoyed to think about what Mom had said and how there was only one boy in the universe who knew my entry in the phone book. So when I pressed the talk button and said hi and Tim's voice came echoing out of the earpiece, I almost hung up in surprise.

"Hey, Cass," he said. "What's up?"

All casual, as if this was your regular everyday phone call. I had to open and close my mouth a few times before my brain got into gear.

"Not much," I said cautiously. Was he really calling just to shoot the breeze? I was a little out of practice with that chatting on the phone thing. Just pretend it's Norris, I told myself. "How about you?"

"Well, I, uh . . . my dad's out of town for the next few days on business. I thought . . . could you help me talk to Mom again?"

Oh. Of course. Stupid for me to have imagined this had anything to do with anything else. "I thought we were done with that," I said.

"Just one more time, okay? All I want is to know that she's still here."

"Of course she's there. Why wouldn't she be?"

"I don't know." He swallowed audibly. "I can't tell, you know. It's not like I can see her or hear her or anything. It seems like she's gone."

"Yeah," I said. "That's normal."

"But I don't want it to be. Okay, I know I'm not going to be able to see her like you do. But when you were talking to her, it was almost like I could feel her standing there."

A board groaned in the hallway. I glanced over my shoulder at the door. Silence. Was that Mom sneaking by, hoping to catch a few words, wondering by what magic a boy had been induced to talk to her daughter? I wasn't going to hear the end of this for weeks. Bad enough that everyone at school was speculating about Tim and me without Mom getting in on it, too.

"So will you come?" Tim asked. "I promise I won't ask again."

Until he started feeling like she was gone again. I thought of Paige, moping in the corner as she waited for Mom to return, just so she could hover nearby without touching, without talking.

"Look," I said, lowering my voice. "I really don't think that's a good idea. You know, your mom wasn't happy about it even the first time."

"Well, we could try. I mean, I'm sure she'd want to—"

"Tim," I said, firmly, "she doesn't want you doing this. And I don't want to be doing it, either, knowing that. All right?"

His voice took on a raw edge. "She'll talk to me. She just doesn't— Look, what do you want? That's what this is about, right? You wouldn't just help me because . . . I told you what I knew about Paul, I took you to the party—I even told Matti off like you asked me to. What else is there? What'll it take?"

There was a catch in my throat, and for a few seconds I couldn't speak. Could he even hear me? I was trying to help him, trying to stop him from . . . from whatever his mom had seen that scared her, and he thought I just needed to be paid off. Well, screw him.

"How about leaving me alone?" I snapped.

Tim's side went quiet for a moment. "Okay," he said,

slowly. "If that's what you want, I can do that. Five more minutes of your time, and I will not come near you again. I will not talk to you, I won't even look at you if you're walking past me in the hall. How's that?"

"That's not—" I caught myself before I could blunder any further. There was a pang in my chest at the thought of Tim passing me without so much as a glance of acknowledgment, but it wasn't as if he would have glanced at me before all this. Things would go back to the way they'd been before, when the worst thing I'd had to worry about was getting Norris and Bitzy back on speaking terms. He was offering me an out. Why the hell wouldn't I take it? Five more minutes couldn't hurt that much.

I remembered the distress on his mom's face and bit my lip. As long as it really was only this one more time.

"All right," I said. "But you have to mean that. This is the last time. You bug me about it again and I'll . . . I'll tell your dad how you've been skipping, and everything."

"Fine," he said. Relief smoothed the anger out of his voice. "You want me to come pick you up?"

Wouldn't that send Mom to cloud nine. "No thanks," I said. "I'll walk. Give me half an hour."

I hung up the phone and leaned back in the chair, listening. Sure enough, there was a creak and the swish of Mom's socks slipping over the carpet as she snuck back down the hall. I walked to the door and peered out. The bathroom door was closing. Good. She mustn't have expected me to make a break for it so quickly.

Sidestepping the creaky spots, I hurried across the hall and down the stairs. To save time, I tugged on my old sneakers with the permanently knotted laces. If I could just get out of here and get this over with, I'd talk to her for an hour when I got home.

The pipes in the wall gurgled. I speed-walked through the living room, tossed a "Going out. I'll be home for dinner," at Dad, and dashed out the back.

"Cassie?"

She was calling from the top of the stairs, but outside I could pretend I couldn't hear. I jogged up the driveway and onto the sidewalk. Home free. I might get an earful when I got home, but at least then I'd have a suitable story. "Just some guy who needed help with the geography homework." Except I'd just used geography yesterday, and that was one course no one would ever ask my help in. "We got assigned to a project together. For, uh, English." That'd do. As long as I wasn't telling her I'd gone off to talk to a dead person, anything would do.

When I reached Tim's house, he opened the door before I had a chance to ring the doorbell. We stared at each other, and my stomach turned over. He looked different, vaguely, like he'd wilted around the edges. His hair lay limp on his forehead with a couple of tufts veering out near the back. If the spiderweb of wrinkles on his T-shirt was anything to go by, he'd slept in those clothes. I could see why his mom was concerned.

It wasn't my fault. I didn't want to be here, doing this, helping this happen. If he hadn't—

"You're here," he said.

I inhaled and pulled myself together. "You were expecting someone else?"

"I wasn't really sure," Tim said. "That you were coming, I mean."

"Have I lied to you yet?"

"Well, no, not that I know of."

He moved over and I stepped inside, scanning the hallway. No dead people there, but the smell of powdered sugar laced the air. I stalked into the living room, and Tim trailed behind me.

"Is she here?" he asked. His hands twitched.

"Somewhere." I turned away. "Mrs. Reed!" I called. "Mrs.—"

She dropped through the ceiling like an autumn leaf and drifted to a stop in front of me, the hem of her dress rippling around her ankles. When our eyes met, and she realized I could see her, her glow flickered in surprise. It'd been three days—no way she'd remember me. Her lips pursed.

"Who are you?" she demanded. "And why are you bothering Tim?"

Great. Yet another person who had this the wrong way around.

"He asked me to come," I said.

"Well, he shouldn't have." She whirled around, her shoulders tensed, like she was about to march out of the room, but she just stood there trembling.

"It's not good for him," she murmured. "I wish I knew how to show him—"

"It's just this once," I said. She was even more upset than last time. I hadn't expected that. "Trust me, I'm not coming again."

"What's going on?" Tim broke in. "She doesn't want to talk?" He stared at the walls, trying to follow my gaze.

"She's worried about you. Like I told you." I jerked my hand toward the sofa. "Sit down. Relax. With you fidgeting like that, it's no wonder she's nervous."

Mrs. Reed raised her voice. "Maybe you can help. Tell him to stop. You have to tell him . . . he has to stop it."

"Stop what?" I said.

She turned her profile to me, gazing across the hall to the staircase. "He has to stop holding on. Stop waiting. I can't come back. He never calls his friends, never talks to anyone. If you saw him. . . . He's not sleeping. All night, he just sits there and looks and waits, and gets up, and wanders, but he doesn't sleep. I can't remember the last time I saw him eat anything. He keeps going to the liquor cabinet, and I know he's drinking. He's making himself sick. I'm his mother, I can tell. He's hurting himself. And there's nothing I can do."

If she'd yanked open Tim's chest and started pointing out his guts to me, I don't think I'd have felt more uncomfortable. Don't tell me this, I wanted to say. It's his business, not mine. He wouldn't want me to know. . . .

Tim stirred, poised on the edge of the sofa, watching me. I had to struggle to swallow.

"What do you want me to do?" I managed.

"I don't know," she said. "If I knew there was someone who could help him—if he could talk to someone, his father, or Nancy—"

I grasped on to the last name like a life preserver. "Nancy's your aunt, right?" I asked Tim.

He frowned. "Yeah. Why? What about her?"

"Your mom thinks you should talk to her. To Nancy."

"What good's that going to do? Aunt Nancy's three hours away—she's got her own kids. Anyway, this has nothing to do with her."

I tried to straighten out everything his mom had said into a coherent explanation. "You know I told you your mom was all concerned about you last time. Well, she still is. More, even. She thinks you're not sleeping and eating enough, that you're looking for her instead of . . . anything else. I guess she figures if you talked to your aunt, you'd feel better, be able to . . . get past this."

"So what—I'm supposed to just forget? Like everyone else wants me to?"

It works for the dead, I thought. "Well, she seems to think you're wearing yourself out. I'm just telling you what she's saying."

Tim slumped, lowering his head into his hands. "Mom, I'm trying, I just can't—" He broke off, his voice ragged. His whole body had gone rigid as if he was trying as hard as he could to hold in tears. A lump rose in my throat.

Instinct told me to turn around, walk away. This wasn't my place. I shifted my weight, then stopped.

I'd stood up to Danielle, to Matti, to a hundred other people over the last few years. Why couldn't I stand up to myself? I didn't like seeing Tim like this. He wasn't a bad guy. In four years, he was the only person who'd bothered to find out what had really happened with Danielle and me. And no matter how many times I'd told him off or shoved him away, he'd taken it and kept coming back. If there was something I could do that would stop him from hurting—

Maybe, this once, I ought to go to him.

I took a step forward, reaching toward him. "Tim," I said.

He exhaled shakily. "What?"

"I—" What could I say? Are you okay? I could see for myself he wasn't. It'll be all right? But it wouldn't be, probably not for a long time.

It wasn't like with Paige or Norris or Bitzy. If I said the wrong thing to them, they'd forget it in a day or two. With Tim, I had to get it right the first time. And I had no idea what right was.

Maybe it was better not to say anything. I uncurled my fingers and rested them on his shoulder with what I hoped was a comforting amount of pressure, watching him, ready to back off if it looked like I was pushing more than helping. He didn't pull away. My mouth opened, and I found myself blurting out the first stupid thing that popped into my head.

"Things are always changing, right? So, even if they really suck right now, eventually they've got to suck less."

Tim let out something almost like a chuckle and started to raise his head. In the same moment, something flickered across the room. My hand slipped from his shoulder as I turned.

Tim's mom was gazing at him, at us, her hair and

dress drifting around her, her lips parting and then, ever so slightly, forming something like a smile. I saw it for only a second before she disappeared.

She didn't dart away or fade out of sight. It was as if her image turned to mist, a million tiny particles suddenly scattered by a breeze. A feeling like static electricity rippled through the air and over my skin. I blinked, and when I looked again, there was nothing left of her at all.

My mouth was hanging open. I couldn't find the wherewithal to close it. Tim stirred beside me.

"What?" he said. "What happened?"

"I . . . don't know." I walked, slowly, to the place I'd last seen her. The room looked no different, felt no different— The smell. I inhaled deeply. My nose confirmed it. Dust, stale coffee, leather—not one speck of sugar.

If she'd only wafted off for a moment, it should still have been strong. The house had been filled with it before, however faint. My room never stopped smelling like Paige's candied apples, even when she'd wandered off for hours.

Mrs. Reed was gone.

"She left already?" Tim was saying. "I thought I still had a little more time. If this is the last—"

"Hold on," I said. I strode into the dining room, the kitchen, the hall, breathing in, breathing in again. More dust, a hint of mildew. Nothing sweet. Without asking Tim if he minded, I bounded up the stairs.

"What is it?" he called after me, panic threading into his voice. "What's wrong?"

I didn't answer. I couldn't answer, not until I knew for sure.

The upstairs hall smelled of aftershave and toothpaste. I opened each door, one by one, and inhaled. Not even a hint of sugar, a lingering so faint I could trick myself into believing it was her. It was as if she'd never been here.

Tim was waiting at the bottom of the stairs. As I looked down at him, nausea swept over me. I could already see how his face would crumple, his jaw quiver, his eyes turn to water. I couldn't stand that. Not here, not now. I had no file on the guy standing before me, on how to handle him or how to deal with this.

I trudged down the stairs, coming to an uncertain halt at the bottom. "She's not here," I said. "I don't know where she's gone. But I . . . I don't think she's coming back. I'm sorry."

"What? What do you mean, not coming back?"

"I'm sorry," I said again, and I really was. So sorry I felt like my insides had tied into one giant knot. "I— There's nothing I can do."

My feet, without consulting the rest of me, shifted toward him, but he stepped back, staring at me. "But she was just here, wasn't she?"

"She was. But she's not now."

He wavered and set his hand against the wall to keep his balance. "She wouldn't just . . . Of course she'll come back."

No, she won't, I thought, but I couldn't bring myself to lay it out so baldly. "Tim, it's—she—"

"You should go," he said dully. He turned toward the door. "You did what I asked you to do. Thank you."

"But—"

"Just go, okay? Whatever you're going to say, I don't want to hear it right now. I have to think." He didn't look at me, just opened the door and stood there, frowning at his hand on the knob. When I didn't move, his voice took on a sharper edge. "Good-bye."

I didn't know what else to do. So I went. I stepped out onto the porch and looked back in time to see the door closing at my heels. I hesitated there in the shadow of the house, the bright spring afternoon just beyond its steps seeming completely unreal.

He wanted to be alone. All right. If nothing else, I could give him that.

CHAPTER 13

My legs might have followed Tim's command to leave him be, but my mind had other ideas. All through dinnertime, my stomach was uneasy, my thoughts restless. I nibbled at my pork chop and rearranged my green beans, kicking at the legs of my chair.

Of course Tim hadn't wanted me to stay. He had to deal with losing his mom all over again—and who was I? Some girl he'd never even talked to a week ago.

I had the feeling deep in my gut that there'd been lines I should have spoken, gestures I should have made, that would have made things better. But looking back, I didn't know what they were. As a friend, I was pretty much useless, apparently.

My throat closed up, and I couldn't swallow the mouthful I'd been chewing.

Mom, with her impeccable timing, chose that moment to start in on me.

"You know," she said as her knife scraped her plate, "I'd like you to be a little more conscientious when you're going out, even if it's for school."

I managed to force the food down. "What?"

"You left today without telling me or your father where you were going or who you'd be with. And you should have told your father exactly where you were going on Friday, too. We need to know these things. You have to be careful."

One second she was overjoyed that I spent two seconds outside of school with someone my age, the next she went all parole officer on me. I didn't have the energy to argue about it. It wasn't like I was planning on attending any more parties. And the chances of Tim inviting me over again. . . . My stomach tightened.

"Sure," I said. "Um, I don't feel so good. Can I be excused?"

"You've hardly eaten."

"Put it in the fridge," Dad suggested. "If you're feeling up to it later, you can have it then."

I thanked him with a weak smile.

Upstairs in my room, I flopped back onto the bed. Mom and her worries. She and Mrs. Reed had that much in common.

I rolled over, curling up with my head on my arm. Mrs. Reed. I'd been trying not to think about that part of the afternoon's events, but there it was. She'd been in the living room, a-gust with worries, and then—what? For no reason, with no warning, gone. Like Chester last summer.

But there had to be a reason, didn't there? Things didn't just happen randomly—the world didn't work that way.

I thought back to that last moment, looking at her before she'd scattered into nothingness. The way she'd smiled. Looking at me, at Tim, at the two of us standing together.

A chill settled over my heart. She'd said she just wanted to know he was okay. To know he had someone who'd be there for him. She couldn't have thought that I would be that person for him, just me? There was no reason for her to trust that I could, or to assume that Tim would want me to—

Why would he, when I was so obviously incompetent?

Paige swooped in through the door, her hair streaming behind her. "Cassie!" she whispered, as if anyone could overhear her. "Did you hear?"

I pushed myself upright. "Hear what?"

She hovered over the desk. "Mom was talking to Dad downstairs—she said the magazine she works for the most is short of money. What if they fire her?"

An easy problem, a problem I knew how to handle. I let out a breath, shakily, and pushed the other thoughts away. "They can't fire her," I said. "She does freelance. I guess they could sort of lay her off, stop giving her assignments, but she's been a regular for years now. They'd get rid of everyone else before her. You know Mom. She just likes to worry."

"I hope so. It sounded like the magazine might just fold. If there's no magazine, nobody's going to be writing for it. They're already making her pay for more of her expenses, she said."

"Maybe she won't be taking off so much of the time, then."

Paige frowned. "I don't like Mom being away, but it's not like I want her to lose her job. She loves it, you know. Can you imagine how sad she'd be—"

"Don't worry," I said. "She'll be fine. She's got lots of connections, right? Even if something did go wrong with this one, she'd still be writing."

"You're right," Paige said, nodding to herself more than to me. "She'll be okay."

I tipped my head back as she floated there, and found myself studying her in a way I hadn't in a long time. As of today, I knew two dead people who'd stayed and then gone. One had stuck around maybe eighty years, and the other, hardly eighty days.

What was the difference? Was it something I had done? Was there something I should be doing for Paige that I didn't even realize?

But I hadn't been anywhere near Chester when he vanished. And . . . even as the thought niggled at me, I couldn't quite believe that Mrs. Reed would have felt comfortable leaving her son in my hands.

Maybe she'd just known he was going to be okay now. Maybe it was him, not me. She'd seen something in him that told her he was coming out of it, that he'd get through. That made more sense. And considering how well my attempt at being a friend had gone, it'd be much better for him.

Oh, please, let that be it.

Paige drifted down beside me. I glanced over at her. If there was something tying her here, the way Mrs. Reed's worry for Tim had tied her—if that *was* what had tied her— I rubbed my forehead with the heels of my hands. Trying to think it through was only giving me a headache. I'd accepted a while ago that there were some parts of death I just couldn't understand, that all I could do was muddle along with what I did know. Nothing had changed that. I'd just added to the list of mysteries.

Still, I couldn't stop the question from slipping out. "Paige, why are you here?"

She stopped short, a couple feet off the bed. "I wanted to tell you about Mom," she said, sounding hurt. "Why do you think?"

"No, I mean here at all."

"What?"

"Well . . ." I grimaced, wishing I hadn't talked myself into this spot. "It's just, not everybody stays, after. Like Grandma McKenna and Grandpa Finch. You don't see them around here. They're just gone. But you *are* here. That's what I mean."

Paige had been twirling a strand of her hair around her finger. Now her hand fell to her lap. "You don't want me here?"

"No, no. Of course I do." I shifted toward her, unable to speak for a second. "I just want to know why. In case . . ." In case I could make her happier. In case I could help her move on, if there was something she was holding on to. I swallowed thickly. I couldn't imagine this room without Paige. To wake up and not have her glow warming the room, her smile lighting up her face . . .

But she wasn't meant to be here. I knew that. The dead were meant to be wherever they all went, eventually.

It would be so selfish of me not to wonder, not to do what I could for her, just because I'd miss her.

"I haven't got a clue," Paige said. "I'm here because I'm here. I didn't decide it. Why are you asking this stuff?"

I didn't figure she'd enjoy the story of Tim and his mom. "What about— Have you ever talked to other people, people like you? Haven't you asked?"

She started sniffling, and I felt like a real jerk. How could I explain that I was only asking this for her sake? I scooted even closer to her, as close as I could get to hugging.

"Cassie," she said, "the only person who talks to me is you."

I pulled up my knees and lay my head on my arms, looking at her. Norris and Bitzy shared a building, knew each other, and still could go months with hardly a word between them unless I intervened. Of course Paige wouldn't think to go badgering some dead stranger for answers. As if any of them had more answers than she did.

"I'm sorry," I said. "I'm just trying to understand."

Paige floated into the corner. She watched me from there, her eyes dark.

"I don't think there's anything to understand," she murmured. "Things just are the way they are." Then she slipped through the wall, and I was alone.

CHAPTER 14

The next morning I went through the motions of eating breakfast and packing my school things, my head in a fog. I'd see Tim at school today. Even if he didn't want to talk to me, I could at least know that he was okay. Maybe now, with his mom really gone, he'd start dealing with it instead of searching for what he'd lost. Maybe he'd start getting better.

I hoped for that so hard my chest ached.

As I walked up to Frazer, I couldn't help glancing over at Chester's ash tree. I broke from the path to the front doors and ambled over for a visit. The pale green leaves fluttered along the branches, which were as skinny as Chester's arms had been. I touched the trunk, running my fingers up and down the smooth bark. There was only silence, me, and the tree.

Chester wasn't coming back. No more shy grin, no more longing gazes at the cars that pulled by, just no more.

My hand dropped to my side. I knew that. Maybe he'd found something, something that had filled a gap that kept him here, something that had released him. With luck, he was happy wherever he'd ended up.

With luck, so was Mrs. Reed.

Inside the school, everything looked the same, sounded the same, smelled the same, but uneasiness prickled over my skin. I hurried up the stairs to the third floor, telling myself it was just nerves and if I ignored them the feeling would go away. It almost did.

Then I stepped out into the hall and saw Norris standing there waiting for me. Not down at the end by my locker like usual. Right beside the stairs, like he'd wanted to catch me as early as possible. He shimmered faintly as he spread out his hands, as if he thought he could block my way.

"I tried to stop him," he said. "I—oh, man, you don't know how hard I swung at his head. I would have pummeled him into a pulp, I swear it, Cass—"

My mouth went dry. The warning bell rang, and the students still swarming around their own lockers grabbed their stuff and started streaming into the classrooms. Even in their hurry, I saw the glances shot my way. I ducked my head and strode past them. It couldn't be that bad. It couldn't be as bad as before. Nothing could be as bad as that.

It wasn't, of course. But in a way, it was almost worse.

I stared at my locker as the last stragglers peered my way, then darted into their classes. The combination lock had been cut; the door hung open a crack. Not enough to see inside, but enough to make me hesitate to open it. The lock itself lay on the floor in front of it, in a puddle of black stuff that seemed to have dripped from within. The same black stuff smeared the edges of the door. Whoever had done this had been very careful not to let a single drop touch the lockers beside mine. This was all for me.

I stepped closer, touched one of the splotches. It was thick and sticky, and when I brought my finger back to my face it smelled like asphalt. Tar. Someone had decorated my locker with tar.

With the same finger, I nudged the door all the way open.

My breath hitched. Tar splattered the inside of the locker, coating the walls and all its contents with a layer of viscous black. A textbook lay open on the stack of things in the bottom. The stuff had been slopped in between the pages and across the cover. It was ruined. Everything in there was ruined. The sweatshirt I'd left when a cool spring day had turned balmy, the binders full of notes I'd need for exams. . . .

My gaze shifted, and for the first time I noticed the inside of the door. The letters painted there had started to run, but I could still read them with no trouble at all.

LAST CHANCE. BACK OFF.

I gritted my teeth. Of course. Who else could it be but Matti? No doubt all Tim's friends stood behind him.

Norris had been hovering behind me meekly, as if afraid of what I'd do to him if he spoke. Now he found his voice. "It was that Matti guy. He came in right after the janitors opened the doors—no one was around—I would have killed him if I could, you know that, Cass—"

"I know," I said, dully. I'd thought things had

changed, but maybe they hadn't. Maybe nothing had changed at all. I was still the creepy girl who'd caught the attention of the wrong guy.

You see? I thought, not knowing if I was talking to Paige, or Mom, or myself. You see? This is why you don't get mixed up in people's lives. Because the living are messy and complicated, and things end up going to hell one way or another, every time.

I shook my head and forced myself to focus. Move forward. Don't let him see he got to me. I had three of my binders in my backpack, another two at home. That only made three classes' worth of notes wrecked. I could survive with the textbooks, and I could come up with some excuse for why I needed new ones. Obviously I'd need to do a little Internet research on how to remove tar—if I could clean this up without all the fuss that would come from the administration finding out, my life would be so much simpler. But now, right now, I maybe had thirty seconds before the bell rang and I was supposed to be sitting at a desk in my biology class downstairs. Another unexplained absence and Mr. Gerry might feel the need to extend his guidance to my parents. The rest could wait.

I pushed my locker closed and rushed down the hall. I was halfway to the stairwell when Tim stepped out of it.

I froze instinctively. As much as I'd worried, as much as I'd counted on seeing him here today, suddenly all I wanted to do was hide. But I was standing in the middle of an empty hall, everyone else already in their classes where they were supposed to be—he would've had to be blind not to see me. He nodded to me, walked over, slowly, and stopped in front of me, teetering like he couldn't quite find his balance. I swallowed. Man, he looked rough.

"Hey, Cass," he said, and rubbed his eyes. It looked like every speck of color from the rest of his face had pooled under them. I hadn't known circles could get that dark.

"You look awful," I blurted out. "You should have stayed home if you're that out of it."

"I'm fine."

His voice said different: It was creakier than the Oldsmobile. He pulled a juice bottle out of his backpack, uncapped it, and gulped, once, twice. The stuff inside had the amber glow of apple juice, but when he lowered the bottle, my nose prickled with the smell of alcohol. He swiped at his forehead with the back of his hand. The fringe of hair there lay on his skin like dead grass.

"Fine," he said, smoother now.

The last bell rang. My hands clenched. Every second that passed now was another second closer to Mrs. Canning finishing off the attendance, sending the folder down to the office with A for absent marked next to my name. But there was no way I could leave Tim like this.

"You'll get suspended, bringing that stuff into the school."

"You going to tell on me?"

"No, but—"

"Good." He dropped the bottle into his bag and jerked his head toward the stairwell. "Let's go."

He reached for my arm, and I dodged him easily. His

aim was so bad he'd probably have missed me standing still.

"Hold on," I said. "Go where? What are you talking about?"

"Home," he said. "We're going home. She'll be back by now, right? I need you to make sure. Don't have to talk to her. Just need to know."

No, she wouldn't be back. She wouldn't be because for some stupid reason she'd apparently decided everything was right in the world, time to move on, when clearly Tim was only falling further and further apart. Why did I have to be the one left to deal with it, standing here with a catch in my throat and no idea what to do?

"Didn't we make a deal that you weren't going to ask me about this anymore?"

Tim smiled faintly. "My dad's gone till Wednesday. You can't tell him anything."

I paused. "I can't tell you anything either. She's gone, Tim. You should go home. Eat something. Get some rest. Stop drinking that crap."

"First you come," he said. "Then I'll do all that. Promise."

"Are you listening? It won't do any good." I touched his elbow, nudging him toward the stairs. "I know this is really hard and you're really upset—maybe if you talked to someone—"

"Don't want to talk. Everyone's been calling. Turned off my phone. As if they give a damn."

"Your mom wanted you to call your aunt. Would you do that?"

He shook his head. "Just come," he said. "Please. Please. Please." His voice broke on the last repetition, and for an awful, gut-twisting moment, I thought he was going to start bawling right there in the middle of school with me. Then he blinked, the teary glint fading from his eyes. He stared down at our shoes, looking as hopelessly lost as one of those Save the Children kids. The light from above hitting his face seemed like it might crack his skin.

My fingers twitched. Part of me wanted to wrap my arms around him, like he really was one of those kids. Hug him and tell him it would be okay, he just had to get through it. But I didn't know how to say that in any way that he'd listen to. The only thing I knew how to do was talk to the dead, and that was what had gotten us into this disaster. And if I gave in again, if I let him keep hoping, he'd end up hurting so much worse in the long run. The sooner he accepted the way things were, the better off he'd be.

"No," I said. "It's not going to happen, Tim. There's no point. She's gone, completely. They don't disappear like that and then come back. Trust me. I can tell the difference."

"You can't know for sure," he insisted. "You didn't look everywhere. You could have missed—"

"I didn't miss anything," I said. "I'm so sorry, I really am, but it's time to give up. Move on, like she wanted you to."

Muffled footsteps tapped over to one of the classroom doors, and a doorknob clicked. A teacher had heard us. I sprang for the stairwell. "Come on, or we'll both get detention."

Tim heaved the door open, and I bolted past him. We raced down to the second floor, Tim stumbling at the bend. I kept going. On the first floor, I pushed through the main entrance and out onto the lawn, the sun hot on the top of my head. Tim staggered out a second later, holding his head with one hand.

"Ugh," he said, sitting down on the steps with a thump.

"Look," I said. "This is everything I know, everything I can tell you. Your mom—for whatever reason—went away, vanished into the netherworld. And when she left, every trace of her left, too. When a dead person's been hanging around somewhere a lot, and you know them like I do, you can tell. There's a sense in the air, a taste, a smell. It stays no matter where they are, and it's really annoying because you can't wash it out of your sheets or spray it away with air freshener. It was gone yesterday. That means your mom's gone. If I could fix things, I would. But I can't do anything. I promise you, I can't."

He peered up at me, wincing in the sunlight. "Why?"

"Because I don't know anything I can do."

"No. Why'd she go?"

"I don't know," I said. It wouldn't do him any good to blurt out the dumb theories that had passed through my mind since then. "Most people, when they die, they go off wherever it is they're supposed to be right away. It just happens. The ones that get stuck here, that's weird. I think, wherever she is now, it's the right place for her. It's better for her to be there than here."

"But, I mean . . . was it my fault? Because I was trying to talk to her? She didn't want to—"

"No. Maybe there wasn't any reason." Maybe she'd thought she was leaving him in good hands. Ha.

"She was smiling," I offered. "When she disappeared. She wasn't worried or upset anymore."

He didn't seem to have heard me. "She's gone," he said to himself. "She's really gone. I don't know what I'm going to do." He gazed blankly across the street. "It's funny, you know. I keep thinking about the stupidest thing. When I was twelve, and my pet gerbil died. It really got to me. But you don't get upset about gerbils when you're twelve. So I acted like it didn't matter. But Mom knew. She came and sat with me and didn't say those stupid things like 'He's in a better place now.' She just said she'd miss watching him scurry across the bars, and I said I'd miss letting him eat seeds sitting in my hand, and I knew it was okay that I was sad."

There was a long moment when I couldn't think of anything to say.

"Of course it's okay for you to be sad. I mean, it's your mom."

"That's not—that's not the way anyone else seems to act. They all made their little pretenses of mourning and then it was supposed to be over, then it was a problem if I didn't want to hang out or party or whatever." He shook his head and then leaned forward until it rested in his hands, rocking ever so slightly. "It's too much. Why did she have to go like that? Why couldn't she have just stayed . . . ? I need her."

The pain in my chest spread as I watched him, an ache that seemed to creep right through my bones. What good was I doing? Nothing I said was making any difference. I was no good at this living-people thing. Talk Bitzy down, cheer Norris up, sure, no problem. The dead were simple, they made sense, that was why I stuck with them.

I'd done what Tim had asked. I'd tried, and now he was miserable.

It would have been better never to have let him get any further than that first day by the lake. Better for him never to have known his mom had slipped through his fingers, and better for me never to have gotten wrapped up in this problem I couldn't solve, this hurting I didn't know how to heal.

Better to walk away now before I made things even worse.

"I've got to get to class," I said. The words sounded awkward coming out of my mouth. "Just . . . talk to your aunt, or someone, please, all right?"

Tim shifted but didn't raise his head. I cleared my throat. "I—I'm going."

I didn't say anything more as I walked up the steps and grabbed the handle of the door. I'd already said far too much. An interesting experiment, mingling with the living, but ultimately one with unfortunate results.

The door thudded closed, and there was only silence behind me. Not a peep from Tim.

I dug my fingernails into my palms and forced myself to keep walking.

CHAPTER 15

All day, between running to classes and trying to clean up my locker, I kept an eye out for that fair head. I didn't see it once. He must have gone home, I told myself. I hoped he was taking the time off to actually recover, and not . . . I didn't want to think about what else he might be doing.

It wasn't as if I had a shortage of things to distract myself with. When I saw Matti, my hands balled into fists, but I kept my cool and simply ignored him. In a couple weeks he would graduate and I'd never have to see him again, anyway. I watched Danielle and Paul in the cafeteria, sitting at opposite ends of the table—Danielle giggling with Jordana, Paul wedged between Matti and Flo and darting looks around the column where he must have been able to see the glint of her hair—and I didn't feel remotely victorious. Paul had been cheating. I'd let Danielle know. Now they were broken up. It probably would have happened the same way without me, just a little later on. It hadn't changed what she'd done, way back when. It hadn't changed anything.

The next morning, I walked through the parking lot

to check for the baby-blue Oldsmobile. It wasn't there. I bit my lip and went into the school.

Norris was waiting by the math office, as usual. I sat down with my back to my open locker, and he squatted down beside me. There was enough time before class that I'd have shot the breeze with him for a bit, but every time I opened my mouth, I saw the parking lot and the empty spot where Tim's car should have been.

"Norris," I said, "could you do me a favor?"

Norris wiggled his eyebrows. "Will I regret it if I say yes?"

"Well, I—" My face got hot.

"Come on, Cass," Norris said. "Like I've got something better to do? What d'ya need?"

"It's going to sound stupid," I said. He shrugged. "I don't know if you remember, but I helped Tim, the VP, out a little, and now— If you could go over to his house, check in on him, just for a couple minutes, so I know . . ." I trailed off. What exactly did I want to know? What would he think, if he knew I was spying on him?

But I had to. If I didn't, not knowing how he was doing was going to drive me crazy.

"You got something on him? Must be good."

"No. It's a long story. He's been kind of messed up, and he hasn't been in school. I just want to know he's all right. Can you do it? You don't have to."

Norris snorted. "Don't worry about it. I'm on it."

I told him the address as the bell rang. He slipped away through the lockers before I'd even closed mine.

Watching him go, my stomach twisted. I wished I hadn't eaten quite so many pieces of bacon at breakfast.

In chemistry class, Miss Taisley had us watch this crazy video about chemical bonding, where all the elements were cartoon people and they chummed up together to form complex substances. I kept expecting it to turn into a giant periodic-table orgy. The lights were off, so when Norris seeped through the door, glowing faintly, I noticed him right away.

He glided over beside my desk, rubbing his hands together. "Mission completed. You want to hear about it now?"

I nodded, pretending to be absorbed by the video.

"Found the guy in the living room," Norris said. "He was lying on the couch. I thought he was asleep at first. And then he called for his mom, but no one came. I didn't see anyone else home. Guess he's sick."

I motioned to my notebook, which had more doodles than notes in it, and wrote, *Was he drinking?*

"You mean booze? I didn't see any. I guess he could have been quiet drunk. Most of the guys I knew, they got wild when they were pissed."

It sounded like Tim wasn't much worse than he'd been on the weekend. Anytime now, his dad would get home, and even if he was a loser he'd have to see something was wrong with Tim and do something about it. I exhaled slowly.

Thank you, I wrote.

"Anytime," Norris said. He hunkered down on the

edge of the desk and watched the rest of the video with me, giving his running commentary about how ridiculous it was.

Walking home that afternoon, I spotted a car in our driveway. Mom had driven to her latest assignment, but she wasn't due back until tomorrow. Coming up the walk, I peered through the side window. That was her pleather makeup bag lying on the passenger seat.

As I straightened up, Mom whisked out the door. The collar of her blouse stuck up on one side and her part was uneven. When she strode down the steps, the hems of her slacks fluttered to reveal one gray sock, one denim blue. All was not well in the world of Mom.

"Inside, Cassie," she said flatly, brushing past me on her way to the trunk. "Sit yourself down at the dining room table and stay there. We're going to talk."

That didn't sound promising. She'd only just gotten home—what could she possibly have to bug me about? Sighing under my breath, I trudged inside.

She made me wait. I slouched in the chair twiddling my thumbs while she lugged her wheeled suitcase upstairs: thump thump thump thump thump. Water ran in the bathroom. She swept by the doorway, her hair fixed, and rattled ice cubes in the kitchen. A key clicked in the liquor cabinet door.

Mom never drank before dinner. We hadn't even started talking and this was already shaping up to be a catastrophic conversation.

I started weighing the consequences of making a

dash for the door. Before I got very far, she breezed into the dining room with all the grace of a hurricane. She set down her drink—her favorite, a Long Island iced tea—and sat with her elbows on the table, her hands clasped in front of her. I watched the ice drift in her glass. It made me think of Tim, Tim and his freezer gin and his stupid juice bottle.

I looked up at Mom and scowled. "You came home early just to talk to me?" I said. "What's the big deal?"

Her mouth tightened, the skin creasing at the corners. "I came home early because the magazine cut my assignment short," she said. "It just happens that the phone was ringing when I came in the door. Your guidance counselor had a few things to say."

Mr. Gerry—that weasel.

"He was particularly concerned about your attendance and your academics," Mom continued. "Apparently you've been skipping a lot of classes."

"That's not true. I haven't missed any since"—since he talked to me about it last week, I was going to say, and then it hit me. I'd missed half of biology yesterday to have that chat with Tim. I slumped back in the chair.

"Mm-hm," Mom said, as if I'd given everything away. "I don't want to hear any excuses. The year's almost over. You've got exams coming up. You'll have the whole summer to avoid school—so do it then."

I threw out the words without thinking. "And you're a good one to talk about avoiding things."

Mom's shoulders stiffened. "What did you say?"

I'd gone too far. I knew it. Even with the frustration

she'd stirred up simmering inside me, I knew it wasn't worth a fight. So I said, "I'm sorry, never mind," and shoved back my chair to stand up. If Mom hadn't pushed it, not another word would have come out.

"Hold it right there," she said, pointing a finger at me. Her hand shook. "I wasn't done yet. To begin with, this attitude of yours. It's disrespectful and spiteful and I want it to stop now."

If she knew, if she had any idea what I'd been going through. . . . I got up anyway, holding it in. I pushed the chair in and stood behind it, gripping the back as if I needed it to keep me on the ground. "Attitude?"

"Yes. This, right now. Playing dumb. Sneaking off. Ignoring us. Don't think your father hasn't noticed, too. You may be sixteen, but I'm still your mother, and I'd like a hello when I get home and a civil response when I ask you something."

How convenient for her to forget that half the time she skipped right over hello and went straight to harassing me. My jaw clenched.

"Maybe if you did more than pick on me, I'd want to talk to you."

"Pick on you?" Her hands leapt into the air and started waving around. "This isn't picking on you, Cassie. This is discussion and discipline. That's my job."

"Oh," I said. "So it's also your job to point out everything that's wrong with me and bug me all the time because I'm not exactly the way you want, I guess."

"Cassie." Her breath hissed coming out. "I'm trying to look out for you. If you go around acting like this your whole life, you'll never make any friends. The colleges won't want you. No one will hire you for a job. You're painting yourself into a horrible, lonely corner. Look at you. You went to school in those grungy clothes, your hair a mess, always frowning. You've got to get out there, put your best face forward, give things a try. Live."

Be like Paige. Be the daughter she really wanted. If it were me dead and Paige standing here, she'd never have had to give a speech like this.

My anger boiled over in a rush of words. "And this thing you're doing, that's living? You never stay anywhere for more than a week, not even here. All you do is complain about the places you went to, about the food that's left in the fridge, about how I'm not good enough."

Her face turned sickly white and her mouth fell open, but I was blundering ahead too fast to stop. The momentum wouldn't even let me slow down.

"It's Paige," I said. "You think I don't know? You pretend like it doesn't bother you anymore, put on your hairspray and your makeup and your perfect clothes, but it's so obvious. It bothers you so much you can't stand to stay here with me and Dad. Where are your friends? Where's your life? You're so busy trying not to think about Paige being dead that you might as well be dead, too."

"Cassie—" she tried.

"No. Shut up. You don't know anything. Maybe the magazine will dump you. You run away from everything. Who wants to hire someone like that? At least I'm not pretending."

I ripped my hands off the chair, my face hot, my eyes

hotter. I bolted out of the dining room and up the stairs, knowing that Mom would screech my name and haul me down to pound a lecture to end all lectures into me.

Except she didn't. Somehow, I made it to my room unsummoned. Sinking onto the bed, I wiped at my eyes and my cheeks. They just got wetter. My heartbeat was hitting my ribs like a hammer. I wondered if blood could break through bone. GIRL KILLED BY HER OWN PULSE. There was a headline Flo'd die for.

I rolled over, staring at the ceiling as the tears streaked down the sides of my face and into my hair. I'd said too much. I shouldn't have. . . . But it wouldn't matter. Mom would just gloss over it like everything else. She'd leave on another trip, and when she came back, it'd be like I'd never said anything. Otherwise she might have to think about what I was saying. As if she'd even consider that

1. I might have a good reason for missing those classes.
2. I might have still had friends if everyone hadn't decided, through no fault of my own, that they wanted nothing to do with me.
3. I might be living better than Paige had. I mean, so far I'd managed not to drown myself. Didn't that count for something?

As I rolled over to bury my face in the pillow, Paige's voice wisped from down the hall. "Cassie!" I wiped at my eyes and sat up just as she slipped through the door.

"Cassie?" she said, gliding over to the edge of the bed. She was twisting her hair around all the fingers of her right hand. If she hadn't been dead and exempt from certain cosmetic laws like roots growing in and nail polish chipping, she'd have ended up with a head full of knots.

She sat very still, but the glow inside her trembled. Guilt rose in my throat. I hadn't thought about her overhearing Mom and me fighting. I'd said those things about Paige. . . .

I coughed, hoping I no longer had that I've-just-been-crying rasp in my voice. "What's up?"

Paige looked down at her hair and her fingers in it and pulled them free. The strands rained over her shoulder and veiled her face.

"Mom's crying," she said. "What happened? Is she okay?"

Mom crying? I couldn't imagine it. I hadn't seen a tear in her eye since Paige's funeral.

"I said some stuff to her," I said, flopping down on my side. "She was laying into me, so I laid it on back."

"Oh, Cassie." Paige sighed her big-sisterly sigh, as if she hadn't shouted at Mom enough times, over boyfriends and which parties she could go to and how late she could stay up: *I hate you! You don't understand anything!*

The only difference was, I meant what I'd said.

"You must have said something really awful," Paige was saying. "I've never seen her this upset. Why don't you apologize?"

If Paige hadn't heard the whole thing, I wasn't going to explain. "I just told her she's away too much," I said.

"And she complains too much. And that's true, so why should I apologize? I was mad at her. People say stuff. It happens."

"I still think you'd better apologize. She looks really hurt."

Maybe Mom ought to feel a little hurt. How did she think I'd felt, left at home all those times, knowing that every time she came back it would only be to remind me how I wasn't living up to her expectations?

I was about to say something like that when the phone started to ring.

CHAPTER 16

A strange thing happened: I picked up the phone. It was probably the first time I'd answered a ring since back in junior high when kids started crank calling and then stopped calling altogether. My arm, without consulting my brain, assumed it was Tim and snatched up the receiver as if the fate of the world might depend on what he had to say.

The last voice I expected to hear was Danielle's.

"Cassie?" she said, before the hello had finished leaving my mouth, and déjà vu washed over me, throwing me back through time to the beginning of seventh grade, before the sneers and the notes and everything else, when a call from Danielle was as ordinary as a pop quiz in math class. I couldn't speak.

"Cassie? That is you, isn't it?" she said. I wrenched myself back to the present. The last time I'd spoken to Danielle, she'd been telling me how pathetic I was. It figured she'd have held on to my phone number all this time anyway, just in case she needed it.

"Yes," I snapped, more sharply than I meant to. I

wrapped my free arm around my belly, holding myself steady.

There was a faint, childish babbling as one of her younger brothers ran by. I wondered if she'd called just to give me the silent treatment.

"Look," she said finally, "I don't want to talk to you either."

"There's a real easy solution for that. Don't dial the number."

"Well, some of us know there are more important things than how much you dislike somebody."

"Great." I scooted back on the bed so I could lean against the headboard. "So tell me about this important thing already, and we can stop talking."

She paused, exhaling. "When was the last time you saw Tim?"

What, was she trying to determine how many claws I'd stuck in him?

"Yesterday," I said.

"Yesterday," she repeated. "So, that was, like, after school?"

"No, first period. What does it matter?"

She ignored my question. "But he didn't come to school yesterday."

"I don't hallucinate much," I said. "That's where I saw him."

"He wasn't in class. No one saw him." She stopped, and I think we both realized the same thing. Tim had come yesterday just to see me. To Danielle, probably, it was just another piece of evidence against me. It couldn't possibly have happened unless I'd voodooed him into coming.

"You haven't seen him since then?" she asked.

"You said the last time. That was it." I figured second-hand seeing by way of dead people didn't count.

"You haven't even talked to him? On the phone?"

"You know," I said, "maybe you could tell me when it became your business how and when I talk to anyone."

"When Tim disappeared off the face of the planet." Her voice wavered. "So have you?"

"No." I frowned at the phone. "What do you mean, disappeared? He's just skipping school, isn't he?"

"If that was it, you think I'd be calling you about it?"

No. I was surprised she'd bothered with me, no matter what kind of trouble she thought he was in.

"Isn't he at home?" I asked.

"I don't know. That's why I'm asking you."

"Well, as far as I know, that's where he'd be. Are we done?"

"Cassie . . . you don't get it, do you?" I could almost hear her nibbling on her lower lip, one of Danielle's few bad habits. "We've been trying to get ahold of him since Sunday. His cell phone's been turned off the whole time. No one's picking up the home line. Jordana and Leon and I even went by and knocked on the door yesterday afternoon, and no one answered."

"He said his dad was away this week," I offered. "Maybe he's enjoying being alone."

"But he wouldn't just ignore everything. Leon's known him for years—he said he's never seen him do anything like this. We left messages telling him we're worried. It's not like him. Something's wrong."

Her panic crept in through my ear and infected my brain. A lot could have happened in the six hours since Norris had checked in on Tim. What if he'd tripped down the stairs and broken all his bones? What if he'd fallen asleep in the bathtub and started breathing water?

Wait. A memory tugged at my thoughts, followed by a cool certainty. Tim had told me he'd turned off his cell because he didn't want to talk—said he didn't believe they really cared, muttered about what jerks his friends were being. Danielle was right, it wasn't like him. Because Tim wasn't like himself anymore. He'd started to see how his friends really were.

Why shouldn't he shut them out, if he wanted to? It didn't mean there was anything wrong with him.

"Maybe he's just not interested in talking to you," I said. "Ever think of that?"

"But . . . we're his friends. Why would he want us to be freaking out—unless—" Her voice hardened. "It's because of you, isn't it? This is your idea."

I started to laugh, but it choked on the way out. "Right. This has to be my fault. It couldn't possibly have anything to do with the bunch of you being rotten people who go around backstabbing each other and ripping people up and tarring people's lockers just for being friendly with someone. He's not blind."

There was a pause. "What do you mean, tarring people's lockers?"

"Oh, come on. Yesterday morning. Matti had to show

I couldn't just push him around, and I'm sure the rest of you were cheering him on."

"I don't know anything about that!" Danielle protested. "So that's why—I thought he looked really smug, but I didn't know why, and if Jordana had, she'd have told me, and Leon and Flo didn't seem to know what was going on. Whatever he did, it was just Matti, not the rest of us."

"Sure, whatever," I said. "Even if that's true, it's just one example. Tim doesn't even know about that—I didn't tell him. He was already fed up with you guys the first time he talked to me. I'm not surprised he's decided to cut you off. I'm surprised it took him this long."

"What? Why? I mean, I know things have been kind of awkward since his mom died, but what do you expect, it's not like—"

"You'll have to ask him when he's willing to talk to you," I said. "It's got nothing to do with me. So, now that we've figured that out, can I go?"

"Wait." She sighed. "I'm sorry Matti pulled whatever crap he did on you. I'm sorry I assumed this was your fault. Can you look past that stuff for a second?"

"What do you want me to see?"

"I called mostly because we—well, some of us—wanted you to try to talk to Tim. To see what's going on. Nothing's changed that."

"Hold on," I said, frowning at the bedspread. "You all hate me, but now you want me to go be friends with Tim? What the hell is that?"

"Don't be dumb," Danielle said, but there was no

anger in her voice, only a terse weariness. "I don't know what's been going on exactly, but there's obviously something with you and him. Something big enough that all of a sudden he's spending more time with you than the rest of us combined. Even if he won't talk to us, we thought he might talk to you. Say whatever you want to him. Just make sure he's okay. That's all we want to know."

Believe me, I thought, remembering how fragile he'd looked yesterday morning, I'd like to know that, too.

"I can't promise anything," I said.

"I didn't think you would."

The phone clicked, and the dial tone beeped in my ear. She'd hung up on me. I should have done that to her in the first place. I slammed the receiver down and shoved the phone to the back of the desk. It figured. Tim had been falling apart since his mom died, and it was only when he shut down completely that his "friends" finally noticed.

"Who was that?" Paige asked from above, and I almost flinched off the bed. I'd forgotten she was there.

"What are you doing up there?" I said, craning my neck. She floated past me and sat on the desk with her legs crossed.

"Listening," she said. "I didn't want to distract you. It sounded pretty intense. So who was it?"

"Danielle. It was Danielle." Now that her voice wasn't in my ear, the conversation seemed unreal. But here was Paige interrogating me about it, so obviously I hadn't imagined the whole thing. It might have taken them a long time, but Tim's crowd must be awfully worried now, if they were resorting to calling me. What if something really had happened to him?

"Danielle?" Paige said, jerking me back to the present. She frowned. "You sounded so mad. I mean, I know you don't really hang out with her anymore, but . . . weren't you two friends? What's going on?"

I stared at her. Of course. We'd never talked about Danielle. She didn't know. Because Danielle had shut me out of her life well before Paige had started taking this new interest in mine, and it wasn't exactly a topic I was going to bring up of my own accord.

"We're not friends anymore," I said. "That's why we don't hang out. It's been a long time; it's not a big deal now."

"But what happened?" She leaned toward me, tipped so far she'd have fallen off the desk if gravity applied to her. "You guys had a fight? Why?"

"It doesn't matter," I said. The day's frustration, from worrying about Tim, from fighting with Mom, from trying to keep ahead of Danielle, it all started to swell inside me. But it wasn't really at Paige, I knew that. I clamped down on it and tried to shove it away. "Look, I just don't want to talk about it."

But Paige had to go into big sister mode. "You get so angry at people, Cassie," she said. "I bet if you talked to her, told her you were sorry, she'd want to be friends again."

"Why are you so sure it was my fault?" I mashed my hands into the pillow. What was with the world today?

"She ditched me, Paige. She was horrible. You have no idea. I wouldn't want to be friends again, even if she by some miracle got down on her knees and begged me to forgive her."

"She always seemed nice when she came over," Paige said doubtfully. "Are you sure it wasn't just a misunderstanding?"

"There's not much room to misunderstand things when your best friend starts treating you like dirt," I said. "I don't care how nice she seemed. She's awful. She made the whole school hate me."

"Why didn't I know that?"

My voice cracked. "Because you were too busy with your own stuff. You made it seem like the most boring chore ever when Mom asked you to spend time with me. I wanted to tell you about Danielle. I wanted to talk to you about everything."

I broke off and closed my eyes, pressing the cool back of my hand against my eyelids. I was not going to cry again.

"You know that for something really important I'd have listened," Paige said. "You should have told me. I'd have tried to help. I know I would have."

I shrugged. It didn't matter anymore. If Paige now was anything like Paige then, maybe she really would have listened. It was too late to find out. "You never really gave me a chance," I said lamely.

"Maybe you didn't give me a chance. You can't expect people just to know things if you don't try to tell them."

"I know," I said. I knew I shouldn't have hated her

back then. I knew I'd shut her out in the end, as much as she'd done to me. "I should have talked to you. And I know you'd rather it was Mom you could talk to now." A wave of emotion washed over me. My stomach felt like it was full of nails, heavy and prickling and hard. I stood up, wavering before I caught my balance. Here I was, moping over four-year-old misjudgments, when Tim was fading away somewhere out there.

"I've got to go," I said. "I just—I need to get out of here for a while."

"Cassie," Paige said, but I turned away and stumbled out the door. Down the stairs, plunging my feet into my sneakers, then through the kitchen and out the back door. The first thing I saw was my bike. I grabbed it and jumped on.

CHAPTER 17

I didn't stop pedaling until I reached the corner of Conway and Nassau, what seemed like a million years later. My head was throbbing. Braking by the corner, I pressed the heels of my hands into my forehead, waiting while my breath slowed. It wouldn't help Tim if I showed up looking like the world was ending.

A nervous twinge fluttered in my chest, but I ignored it. In the midst of her ranting, Danielle had made a good point. Tim had come to me over everyone else. Even if I wasn't quite what he needed, even if I couldn't make up for his mom disappearing—I had to think maybe he'd *want* to see me. To know I at least wanted him to be all right.

Pushing off again, I rode the last few blocks to Tim's house at a slightly less panicked pace. When I got there, I rode up on the sidewalk and dropped the bike on his lawn. My heart sank. The Oldsmobile was gone. The space on the street in front of his house was vacant, and the driveway, too. I snuck around back to check the garage. The squat brown building hardly looked big enough for the Olds to fit. Peering through one of the dirty windows, I saw dust floating in a streak of sunlight, a couple of paint cans, a rusty tool box, a rake, and the bare cement floor.

The chances of Tim's car being gone without Tim in it, I figured, were about as slim as the chances of Danielle falling passionately in love with Mr. Minopoplis.

Just in case, I climbed up the porch steps and pressed the doorbell. As I waited for the response I didn't think would come, I glanced in through the door's window. Nothing moved inside. The house was empty. But there was something standing in the middle of the kitchen floor.

I squinted through the shadows. It was a wine bottle. Its base was ringed with dark liquid. Otherwise it was as empty as the house.

My breath stuck in my throat. The image formed in my mind, as clear as if I was seeing it: Tim sitting there on the floor just a couple hours ago, while I was sitting in my chair in class, the level of the wine dropping gradually from neck to base with every gulp. And then he'd headed out for a drive. The way he drove even when he was sober, he'd be lucky if he wasn't bent around a tree, or crushed into the side of another car, or trapped at the bottom of the lake.

Maybe he was.

My stomach turned over as if I'd been the one drinking too much. I sank down on the top step and covered my eyes. He was such an idiot. What was I supposed to do now? Bike around the city looking for him? He could be anywhere.

Did it matter? I was too worried not to try.

I swung onto my bike and headed down Nassau. When I reached the end of the street, I looked both ways and decided to work my way down toward the lake. I'd been through a lot of the area to the north already.

Little kids were racing along the sidewalks on scooters and tricycles, shouting to each other over the rattling wheels. The sun beamed through the deep green leaves of late spring. It was one of those days that's supposed to feel like nothing bad could possibly happen. My pulse was all over the place, one second racing, the next almost stopping as I turned the corner, bracing myself to see a blue car crumpled in the street. Just another line of SUVs—not an Olds in sight. My heart started thudding again.

No one could say I wasn't thorough. I wove carefully up and down the streets, and it was past dinnertime when I caught my first whiff of the beach breeze. People were barbecuing on the park grills, and the air tasted like charcoal and freshly seared burgers. My stomach grumbled. The sun was dipping down, almost touching the roofs of the two-story houses, and my calves were starting to ache from pedaling.

Just a few more streets, and I'd hit the lake. I had no idea where I'd go after that.

I'd almost reached it when I heard the honking. A stretched-out *beeeeeeeep* screeched through the rows of houses, and I flinched in my seat. Somewhere down near the beach, tires squealed as they jerked off course. Then another *beep-beep-beeeeeeeep*. A man bellowed, "Get out of the road, buddy!"

Veering around the next corner, I headed straight for the lake. The back of my neck prickled as I scanned the streets. The honking got louder. Abruptly, the road ended and I found myself on Lakeside Avenue, the last road between the city and the park. I braked, half standing on the pedals to see over the tops of the parked cars.

A guy was standing in the middle of the road with his back to me, just up Lakeside. I didn't see the Olds anywhere, but the guy was too tall, too pale, and too skinny to be anyone but Tim. He waved at the cars as they beeped and swerved around him, stumbled to the side, caught himself, and swayed to the other. "Piss off, you maniac!" someone yelled from a sports car as it whipped past him. Tim's hair rippled.

The traffic lulled for a second, and I dashed to the other side of the street, where the curb was clear. Dumping the bike, I ran up the sidewalk.

"Tim!" I shouted. "Tim!" Over and over. I didn't know what else to say. If I'd stopped, I think my throat would have burst and I'd have just screamed.

The fifth or sixth time I called his name, he swiveled around. I stopped on the sidewalk across from him, hovering on the edge. He looked at me, and his mouth slid into a crooked smile. "Well, here's Cass," he said. Then, to the ancient sedan puttering around him, "That's Cass." The woman driver gave him a frightened look and sped away. "Why doesn't anyone want to play?" he said, throwing his arms in the air.

"Tim," I said. My breath rasped between my words. "Could you . . . come over here? For a second?"

Miraculously, he came. At the curb, he staggered and I caught his arm. His palms were scratched and flecked with gravel. Sometime earlier, there hadn't been anyone to catch him. He looked at me sideways, his head drifting.

"What are you doing?" I said, my voice shrill. "Are you crazy? You could have gotten killed."

Tim yanked his arm away. "What's it to you?"

"What are you talking about? Look, snap out of it, all right? This is just stupid."

"You said I could have gotten killed," he said, slowly. "What would that matter to you?"

As if I'd spent the last two hours looking for him so we could debate my right to speak to him.

"Don't be an idiot," I snapped. "I don't want you to die. You think I need more dead people in my life? Y'know, I bet someone's called the police on you. Why don't we go—"

"No," he said. "I'm not going anywhere with you."

The guy chases me around the city all week, and now that I actually want to do something for him, I've got cooties. Perfect.

He made like he was going to walk back onto the road, so I stepped in his way. "Sorry, I'm not giving you a choice."

For a long moment, he just stared at me like I had antennae poking out of my head. Then he blew out a breath. "This," he said, "is very annoying. All I am trying to do is commune with the cars. Don't know why you're here. Never seemed to want to go anywhere I was before. I wanted . . . I thought we could be friends, or something, but you've made it perfectly clear you've got better things to do. Besides, you told me things can't go back, she won't come back—so I'm going to her. Why the hell are you stopping me? Trying to make my life even more miserable?"

I sputtered before I could speak. "You'll be a lot more miserable if one of those cars runs you over. And I never said I had 'better things'—why would you even . . ."

The words jumbled in my head as what he'd said sunk in. All right, so I'd given him a hard time about a lot of things. What did he expect? Did he not know that I was doing ten times more for him than I'd done for anyone alive in years? I wasn't talking to anyone else at all. I wasn't contacting anyone else's dead relatives for them. I certainly wasn't racing all over the city trying to save them. If I wasn't avoiding them, I was ripping them to pieces. I could have had the whole school laughing at him, embarrassed him beyond belief, couldn't I? But I hadn't.

So how could he seriously think I hated him?

"You see?" Tim said. "I told you." He turned away and slogged up the sidewalk like he was walking through mud. It wasn't hard to catch up.

What had Paige said? *You can't expect people to know things if you don't tell them.* Was that all this was about—I had to spell it out for him?

Well, it was worth a try. My current tactics were getting me nowhere.

"All right," I said, keeping to the side as he wavered to and fro, "so I wasn't the friendliest person ever. But what about everything else?"

"What else?"

"I helped you find your mom and talk to her. Three times."

"So I'd stop bugging you," Tim said. He lurched around a strolling couple and whacked his shoulder on a telephone pole. He didn't even wince.

"That's not the only reason. And I didn't tell anyone at school about the crazy stuff you were doing."

"Because you thought I'd tell them what *you* do."

And he accused *me* of being difficult. "What about this?" I said. "I'm here, aren't I? I went by your house because I was worried about you. And when I saw your car was gone, I was worried enough that I went looking for you. Why would I do that if I wanted nothing to do with you?"

He paused, leaning on the outer railing of the beach parking lot. On the far side, the Oldsmobile sprawled over three parking spots. I guessed it was lucky the car had made it into the lot at all.

Tim swayed and sat down on the railing, his face damp with sweat. His skin looked translucent, traces of red and blue showing through where the blood vessels brushed close to the surface. His jaw clenched. He twisted, suddenly, and leaned over the corner of the lot. I glanced away, squeezing my eyes shut. His breath hitched, and vomit splattered the pavement.

I didn't look until I heard him straightening up. He slumped forward, his arms resting on his knees, but a light flush of color had come back to his cheeks. I stood there, awkward, as he stared at the sidewalk. When he finally glanced up, his gaze seemed steadier.

"I don't know," he said, his voice rough. "Why are you here?"

"I told you," I said. "I was worried. Danielle called me saying everyone was freaking out and no one could find you. She asked me to try to get ahold of you. You know how I feel about Danielle—if I wasn't worried enough on my own, there's no way I'd have done something for her. But I was worried. I wanted to know you were okay."

Tim lowered his head. He rubbed the back of his neck. "No," he said. "I don't believe you. There's got to be some other reason."

He got up and took a few shaky steps into the parking lot, testing his balance. "It doesn't matter," he called, without looking back at me. "I'm going to get in my car and drive into a tree, or off a bridge, and then I'll see Mom again, and not all the pricks around here, and it'll be better like that."

"Whoa!" I scrambled over the railing, too fast. My foot slipped, and I wrenched my shoulder as I caught myself against a post. Hissing at the pain, I ran after him.

"How's that better?" I said, coming up beside him. "Maybe you see her, maybe you don't—I don't know, so there's no way you can. And you lose everything else. Really, I've talked to enough of them. No one's happier being dead."

He shrugged. "What's there to lose? I thought . . . I was dumb. If I wasn't VP, if I didn't know the right people, no one would even talk to me. Everyone's doing it for themselves, no one thinks about anyone else. I don't want to be in that. I'm sick of it."

I tried to step in front of him, but he pushed right past me, aiming straight for the car. He was really going to do it. The breath gushed out of me like someone had bashed my chest in with a sledgehammer. I grabbed his elbow.

"Look," I said. "You want proof it's not everyone? It's not me. I'm not here because of who you are or who you know. You want me to say I messed up? I did. I was as full of crap as the rest of them. Everyone was falling all over themselves for you, and I wanted you to know I wasn't like that. So I was a bitch. That doesn't mean I—"

Heat washed over my face and welled in my eyes. I choked on the words. Ducking my head, I let my hair slide over my face. This was not a good time to be a flake. I had to think, not get weepy.

"What?" Tim said, suspicious. "That's it?"

He'd stopped. I was going to make a fool of myself, but he'd stopped walking. Well, hadn't he almost cried in front of me enough times? To hell with it. I steeled myself and raised my chin. The world looked watery, but the breeze cooled my cheeks.

"You want someone to really care?" I said. "I care. All right? I haven't liked anyone who wasn't dead for four years. I'm out of practice. I acted like a jerk. But I'm telling you now. That's got to count for something." I wiped at my eyes. "Anyway, it won't count if you go and kill yourself."

Tim wasn't moving toward the car, but he wasn't saying anything either.

"You're right—I thought everyone was a creep and a

poseur, and there was no one worth liking," I said, trying to smile. "But I admit it, I was wrong. Could be you are, too."

His head drooped. "I don't know," he said. He sounded wiped. "I feel dead already."

"That'll happen when you down a whole bottle of wine."

"There's more in the car." He took a step forward, but I was faster. I marched over to the Oldsmobile and propped myself against the driver-side door.

"You're not getting in," I said.

"What if I just want to go home?" he asked, eyeing me. Wondering, probably, if he could drag me off it.

"Like you're sober enough that I'd trust you not to drive into a tree by mistake." Suddenly I wished I'd let Mom convince me to get my license when she'd given me the "you'll have to learn eventually" speech a few months back. "Call a cab. Take the bus. Walk. I'm going nowhere."

He jingled his keys in his pocket. When he drew out his hand, it was empty. After a moment, he reached out and touched my hair, like he was making sure I was really there.

"If you mean it," he said, "you won't tell anyone, right? I don't want . . . I don't want you talking about this with my crap friends, with my dad . . . never with my dad." His voice shook. "You have to promise."

"Tim—"

"Promise!"

I drew in a breath. There was no way I could know he wouldn't drown himself in another wine bottle tomorrow and take a drive somewhere I couldn't find him. My friendship wasn't enough to solve a problem this big. I knew I had to go to someone else—but I could still make this promise.

"Okay," I said, carefully. "I promise not to tell your friends or your dad."

For a moment we just looked at each other. Then he turned away.

I stuck close to the car as he shuffled across the parking lot and down the street. My ears pricked for the sound of honking. Ten minutes passed with only the whir of the cars rushing by. I started to relax, but I didn't leave. The Oldsmobile's shadow crept out under my feet, and mine touched the wheels of the minivan four spots over. An ice cream truck jangled by after its last trip past the elementary school yard.

It was almost summer. I'd lost my sense of time. The last week felt like it should have been a year.

Gingerly, I pushed myself upright. My shoulder ached from when I'd almost tripped, and there was a pang of guilt in my stomach for Mom and Paige. Somehow I'd expected there to be a hole, too, a vacant space left by everything I'd spilled to Tim. Instead, I felt all right. If I hadn't still been worried about Tim, it might even have felt good.

When the sun hit the trees on the other side of the lake, I found my bike and headed home.

CHAPTER 18

By the time I got to the house, it was after eight, but it looked like Mom had just started dinner. I saw her through the screen door, leaning over the stove. The smell of basil and tomatoes wafted onto the porch.

She glanced up as I came in, and her spoon clanged on the inside of the pot. I felt myself gearing up to go into casual mode: say hi, kick off my shoes, and act like nothing had happened. I steadied myself. The air was heavy and the silence awkward, because something *had* happened.

"Cassie," Mom said, coming to the doorway. She had a spot of tomato sauce on her cheek and a pinkish tinge around her eyes.

We looked at each other for a minute, feeling out the space between us. Then I said, quietly, "I'm sorry."

Mom nodded. "I'm sorry, too."

"I didn't mean all of it. Some of it I did, but I know some of it wasn't fair. I was really mad."

"Well," she said, "we waited on dinner for you. Why don't we eat, and afterward we can talk about the parts you did mean. Okay?"

I breathed in. The air felt lighter. I could do this, and then I could do what I had to for Tim, and maybe everything would be okay. "Sounds good," I said.

After dinner, Dad took care of the dishes while Mom and I sat down in the living room.

"Why don't you go first," Mom said. She smiled, a little stiffly. I couldn't blame her if she was nervous about what might come out of my mouth. I was nervous.

"I—" I swallowed. Now that I wasn't angry, it was harder to say any of it to her face. I'd been holding the feelings inside for so long, it was like they had grown into me, and I had to pull them out by the roots. "I feel like you're hardly ever here. And then when you are here, you're on my case a lot. Like you don't like the way I am. But this is just . . . the way I am. Maybe if you were around more, you'd see I'm okay."

Mom's face had relaxed. "You think I want you to be more like Paige was," she said.

"Yeah, it seems that way."

"Cassie." She sighed. "Paige wasn't perfect. There were things I got on her case about, too."

"But she had lots of friends," I said. "You're always bugging me about making friends."

"Well, Paige lost the chance to do a lot of things. I suppose I'm afraid you'll miss out, too, because you won't give yourself the opportunity."

When she put it that way, I could kind of see her point.

"You don't have to be as social as Paige," she continued. "But you do seem to spend a lot of time here alone."

"You bug me about other stuff," I pointed out. "Like where I went on the weekend."

"I can't help being a little overprotective. I am your mother." She shifted closer and put her hand over mine. "I don't want you to think I'm disappointed in you. I'm not. I just want you to be as happy as you can be."

I wanted to tell her that I was happy, but right then, I wasn't really sure. What was happiness anyway? That good feeling when I'd first gotten the dirt on Paul? That had faded so fast. How could I know if I was happy if I didn't even remember what it felt like?

In the pause, Mom said, "I talked to my editor at *Travel Insight* a couple days ago, about taking fewer away assignments. I'll be home for the next few weeks. What if I promise not to criticize you about anything for the first week? We'll take some time to get to know each other again."

"Okay," I said. "I'm going to remind you if you slip up though."

"Of course," she said. "You know, I'll still be traveling sometimes. Maybe during the summer you could come with me and see what it's like."

"Maybe." I'd been annoyed at Mom for staying away, but now the thought of her being around made me feel twitchy. I'd gotten used to it being just me and Dad. But I guessed it'd work out if she really did start acting like a mom and not like a prosecutor. She seemed like she was trying anyway. That was something. Maybe . . . I could try to be less harsh on her, too.

Afterward, I trudged upstairs to my bedroom. I

hesitated for a moment, then sat on the bed and lifted the phone onto my lap. My hand shook as I picked up the receiver.

I'd gone over this in my head a million times in the last hour. I couldn't follow Tim around for the rest of his life, jumping in front of him whenever he tried something stupid. I couldn't get his dad involved—I'd promised that much. But Tim had sounded like he liked his aunt, and his mom had encouraged him to go to her.

Trouble was, I only had her first name, and Tim wasn't likely to hand any information over to me. But . . . he'd said she'd stayed with him while his mom was sick. His friends had probably met her. There was a chance she'd have given them some way of contacting her. Or that at least they'd know more about her, so I could figure it out for myself.

Steadying myself, I dialed the number I'd never quite managed to unmemorize.

Someone picked up on the second ring. "Hi, Cassie."

My breath hitched. Caller ID, I reminded myself. But between my nervousness and the sharpness of Danielle's voice, a snappy response popped out before I could bite it back.

"I've been going by Cass for a while now. Maybe you didn't notice."

"Is that why you're calling? To tell me how to say your name?"

"No, I"—I forced myself to inhale—"I need to talk to

Tim's aunt. Nancy? She stayed with him before. I thought maybe—if any of you have her phone number, or know where she lives—"

"Why?" Danielle broke in. "What happened? Is he okay?"

"Yeah," I said, hoping that was true right now. "I just—it's complicated. I can't get into it."

"Why not? You can't just ask for stuff like that and—"

My fingernails dug into my palm. "Danielle," I said, "I want to talk to Tim's aunt Nancy. That's all there is to it. Can you help me or not?"

For a long moment, dead air hung between us. I backed down too many times before, I thought. I played by the rules you made. This once, you can do something for me.

She broke the silence first.

"Okay," she said. "I think—I think she gave her cell number to Leon, just in case. Hold on while I call him. I'll call you right back."

"Sure," I said, with more warmth than I'd expected to muster. "Thank you."

It took only a minute before the phone rang again. "Ready?" she asked, and rattled off the number. I stared down at my scrawl on the back of the notebook I'd grabbed, my heart thumping.

She paused. "You know, Cassie—Cass—I am sorry about what happened in junior high. I didn't mean for things to end up the way they did. I was mad, and I did some rotten things, and then everyone else joined in, and it just got crazy. After a while, I wasn't even angry any-more, but it wasn't like it was up to me what they did, you know?"

"All right," I said. There was nothing more I could say to that.

We held there for a minute, not enemies, just two people, and I thought, now it's done.

Almost.

I had one more call to make.

The next morning, I woke up so early only the faintest gleam of sunlight was peeking through my window. My heart was thumping, suddenly uncertain. I tried to hold on to the memory of my conversation with Tim's aunt, the reassurance that had been in her voice, but the ques-tions flooded in anyway.

What if Tim hadn't even made it home last night? What if he'd come back for the car before he'd completely sobered up? I should have stayed, I should have gone with him, I should have—

I rolled over and pressed my face into my pillow. I was only one person, and calling his aunt was the best thing I could have done. She'd said she was coming down today to see him. That had to be enough.

If only I could be sure he'd see things that way, too. He'd been so intense, so insistent that no one know. What if I'd made things worse all over again?

I bit my lip and dragged myself out of bed.

The worries followed me to school, a lump in my throat and a knot in my stomach. I might as well have slept through my classes—everything the teachers said seemed to float right by me. By the time final bell rang, it was all I could do to remember which locker was mine. I twisted the wrong combination three times before I finally got it open. Norris sauntered over as I stared inside.

"Hey, Cass," he said, slicking his palm over his hair, "I've got a pretty wild one. The principal, right, he—"

I swallowed hard. "Norris, I don't think I want to hear dirt on people today." I paused, and the realization hit me with a sweeping sense of relief. "Actually, I don't think I want to hear stuff about anyone, anymore."

Norris gaped at me. "What? But—you have your mission. Calling them on the crap, making them face up. You're just giving that up?"

"I've got enough other things to think about," I said. "Anyway, how many of them stopped being jerks because of me?"

"Okay, not so many. But, man . . . there goes the excitement out of my afterlife."

"You can still spy on them all you want. I just don't want to hear about it. And we'll still talk." I managed a thin smile. "I've got contemporary history next year. You can help me with my homework."

"Right. Straight from the source!"

When I didn't respond, he slipped partway through the locker, so he could look at me face-to-face, and cocked his head. "Are you okay, Cass?"

"I'm fine," I said.

Except I was about as close to fine as the Antarctic was

to New York, and I knew it. Why was I lying? To impress some dead guy with my deathly cool? Since when had I been such a poseur?

I wasn't sure I wanted the answer to that.

"You sure?" Norris was saying. " 'Cause no offense, but you don't look so sharp."

I shook my head. "No, you're right. It's just, this guy I'm kind of friends with, he was talking really seriously about . . . about killing himself, yesterday. So I'm stressed. A lot."

"Whoa," Norris said. "You think he'd really do it?"

"He was already trying to. I don't know if he'll try again. I told someone, even though he didn't want me to—I think she'll make sure he gets help—but he proba- bly hates me now."

Norris shrugged. "Better angry and alive than just plain dead, right?"

I leaned against the neighboring locker and rubbed my eyes. "Yeah. Of course. I just—"

I just cared. There was nothing wrong with that, was there?

And as a person who cared, surely there was nothing wrong with happening to wander by his house, just to see if, well, there was anything to see? Check that his aunt had come by, make sure he'd survived the time since I last saw him, that he was in good hands now.

"What?" Norris said, and I realized I was smiling for real now.

"Nothing," I said. "Just—I've got to get going. See you tomorrow!"

My heart raced me down the stairs, threatening to burst out of my chest. I half walked, half jogged home, where I grabbed my bike and took off for Tim's place. As I rounded the corner onto Nassau, my breath stopped.

The Oldsmobile was parked out front. In one piece. That meant chances were Tim was still in one piece, too.

I braked across from the house. He might already be gone. His aunt could have come, picked him up—

Then I saw the back of a head and the sheen of light blond hair through the living room window. My pulse hiccuped. Someone was sitting on the couch, just inside. I hesitated, and in the same moment, the head turned to look outside. Our eyes met.

Tim's face tensed. He got up and walked out of view.

I wavered on the sidewalk for a minute longer. Tim didn't come back. I knew he was home, at least, and not in a hospital. I could leave.

Instead I set my bike down on a lawn and went across the street to his house.

Moments after I rang the doorbell, the wooden inner door creaked open. Still half behind it, Tim stared out at me. It wasn't quite a glare, but there wasn't anything friendly in it either. His skin looked sallow, his fingers spidery thin.

"Hi" was the best I could come up with.

Tim said nothing. He moved forward, and I backed up as he came out onto the porch.

"Did your aunt come?"

"She's on her way," he said. "She's driving me up to stay at her place for a few days."

"Oh. Good." That was good, right?

"She seemed to think it wasn't safe for me to drive myself." He paused. "You called her."

I couldn't see any point in denying it. "I was worried," I said. "I didn't know what else to do."

"You could have left it alone. I asked you—you promised—"

"With your dad and your friends. I didn't say anything about her."

"You knew I meant everyone." He closed his mouth tightly, his eyes challenging.

I couldn't breathe, but I refused to lower my gaze. "It was more important that you stayed alive."

"Funny, I'm not really convinced."

"Look," I said. "I know you're pissed at your friends, and you feel like everyone sucks, and I know what that's like. But it isn't everyone. You have your aunt. You have— well, you have me, if that matters. There are tons of people out there who aren't Paul or Matti—you can make new friends, better friends. It'll get easier."

"Do you even believe that?" he asked. "You think the whole world's full of crap. You told me."

"Yeah, and I also told you I was wrong."

"So I'd do what you wanted."

"And because it's true."

He raised his eyebrows. "So you're going to go out there and start making friends, too, then? Actually talk to people at school, find out more than just the stupid things they've done?"

"I . . . I guess." I hadn't thought that far; even the idea of trying to shoot the breeze with any of my classmates sent a shiver of panic through me. I pressed on. "I'm not getting dirt on people anymore."

"So what you're saying is you're actually talking to people *less* now."

"What does it matter?" I said. "This isn't about me. This is about you. I'm not the one walking into traffic."

"Of course this is about you," he said tersely. "You're the one telling me life's worth living, people aren't so bad—that me being alive is more important than people thinking I'm crazy. How can you tell me I have to try when you won't?"

"I am trying," I said. "I'm here. You want me to talk to every person I see at school tomorrow? Fine. I will, if that means you'll stop talking like this and try, too."

"Would you really?" he said. "Or would you chicken out?"

My hands clenched. "Look," I said, not knowing exactly what was going to come out until I heard the words, "I would go to prom if it meant I knew you'd be okay. All right?"

He eyed me quizzically, and his lips quirked. "Now I really don't believe you."

"You want to bet on it? Come. I'll be there."

We held each other's gaze for a few seconds longer. He looked away first. I couldn't tell whether what I'd said had made any difference at all.

I grasped at the only thing I had left.

"You know," I said, haltingly, "your mom—" His head jerked up, and uncertainty tightened my throat. "I told you I don't understand how these things work. But, when she disappeared, she really was smiling. It was when I was trying to . . . to tell you things would get better. I don't think she could have let go if she hadn't believed you could get through this, that you had people who'd help you."

"Are you saying Mom disappeared because she thought you'd help me?"

"No. I don't know. There were probably all sorts of factors. And she probably didn't have control over any of them. But I think that was at least a little piece."

His hand tightened on the porch railing, his knuckles whitening. "But why did she—"

"That's not the point," I broke in. "It's not about why she disappeared. There's no way we can know that. With the dead"—Paige's words, from when I'd asked her almost the same thing, echoed in my mind—"with the dead, things just are the way they are. I know you miss her, and maybe this doesn't make anything better, but she was happy right then, and—"

"I can't talk about this anymore," he said abruptly, turning away.

"What?"

"I don't want to talk. Not about her, or about you, or any of this. You don't know anything about her. Okay? Just . . . just go away."

He stepped inside. The screen door closed behind him, and he walked down the hall without looking back. I heard his dad's voice, faintly, and backed down the steps.

He'd be okay, I told myself. His aunt was coming, he'd accepted that. She'd find a way to help him. I'd done that for him.

And he hated me.

I dragged in a breath and hurried to my bike. Pushing off, I pedaled as fast as my feet could take me until the wind made my eyes water.

CHAPTER 19

Tim didn't show up at school for the rest of the week, but I knew he was at his aunt's place, and the gnawing worry faded to an insistent nibble. Friday afternoon, all of Frazer piled into the auditorium for the traditional end-of-the-school-year assembly. I watched the student council run through their skit, without Tim, and wondered if I'd see him again. Would he come back for exams? Would the principal give him an exemption? He was graduating, in theory. Moving on.

Maybe that last glimpse of him I'd gotten, of his back as he retreated, was the last I'd ever have. The thought felt like a block of ice in my stomach. As long as he's all right, I told myself. That's what matters.

But it wasn't all that mattered to me.

It wasn't until later that night, as I was attempting to study for Monday's chemistry exam—which at the moment mostly involved speculating about how Tim was getting on at his aunt's, and how long he might continue to hate me for sort of breaking my promise—that I thought about the other promise I'd made. I was searching my desk for a pencil sharpener with Paige helping me from above, and I opened the drawer I'd tossed the prom ticket into. My hand fell to my side. I stared at the ticket, remembering the challenge I'd flung out. *Come. I'll be there.*

Paige locked onto it a second later.

"Cassie!" she shrieked. "You're going to prom? Why didn't you tell me? That's amazing! When is it?"

"Next Friday," I said. My mouth had gone dry.

There were a million reasons not to go. For starters:

1. I had probably called out half the people who'd be there at least once. Therefore,
2. half the people who'd be there hated me, and
3. I'd be stuck at a table with at least a few of them. Talk about uncomfortable. Not to mention,
4. if forced to dance, I'd trip over my feet after two steps and break my neck. All of which suggested,
5. I'd have a much better time staying home clipping my toenails.

But there was one huge factor that outweighed all that. I'd promised Tim I'd be there. I'd told him to come so I could prove it. And I really, really hoped he would.

I ran my finger around the edge of the ticket, my stomach twisting. But the point wasn't really whether he'd know or not, was it? Maybe he was right. Maybe I shouldn't have been telling him to give life another chance when I hadn't even taken the chance to say hi to anyone at school. Did I really want to be the same me who'd ripped into Tim that first day when he'd asked for my help, who had assumed the worst of everyone?

I had to go. Because I'd promised Tim. Because the me I wanted to be would be brave enough to give it a try.

"Would it be too weird if I went alone?" I said. "I mean, I don't need a date, or something like that . . . ?"

"Don't be silly," Paige said. "A bunch of my friends went stag. Everybody does it."

I smiled crookedly. "I don't even have any friends to go with." Maybe only half of the people there would hate me, but the rest didn't even know me.

"So what? You go and eat and dance and have fun, for you. Maybe you'll make friends while you're there. Whatever. Since when do you care, right?" She gave me a ghostly nudge. The humor in her eyes faded when she saw I wasn't smiling anymore. "I mean, you don't have to go."

"No," I said. "I should. I will. I just . . ." The feelings were too tangled to be forced into words.

She sank down onto the bed beside me. "What if I went with you? Then you wouldn't be alone."

I stared at her, trying to figure out if she was joking again. She looked serious. Not for the first time, I wondered if she remembered any of the things we'd said to each other on Wednesday about who'd let down who. She couldn't; it'd been too long. But I almost wished she did.

"You want to?"

"Puh-leaze," Paige said, rolling her eyes. "When have I ever *not* wanted to go to a dance? Now let's go tell Mom."

I started laughing. In that moment, it all seemed easy.

When Mom finished picking her jaw off the floor, she was already babbling about the lovely dress boutiques she could take me to.

"Nothing too fancy," I warned her. "You try to stick a sequin on me and I will run away screaming."

In her role as cosmetics instructor, Paige spent every spare moment of the weekend lecturing me about face powdering and arguing about my shade selections when she followed me to the drugstore.

"That one, there, Ruby Rouge," she said, pointing at the lipstick display. "It'd look amazing on you."

It'd make me look like a hooker, I thought, but I couldn't say that with the saleslady hovering at the end of the aisle. I shook my head and picked up Nearly Nude.

Paige sighed. "Oh, come on. This is probably the only time I'll get lipstick on you all year—I want people to be able to tell you're wearing it."

After an extended, half-mimed negotiation, we compromised on a light maroon gloss.

The day of, Mom bustled me off to the salon and told the hairdresser, "Do what you can with it." He heaped the mess up on top, iced it with gel, and swirled it around. It looked like I had a mud sculpture sitting on my head, but Mom was happy. I guessed it was better than the limp, stringy mud I'd had hanging in my face before.

Paige liked it, too. "You look gorgeous," she declared after we'd finished making me up, fifteen minutes before takeoff. I think she was exaggerating just a little. "You know, your hair looks really good up."

I touched the nape of my neck gingerly. It felt so . . . bare. Well, it wasn't like Tim was going to come swinging an ax at me. I was probably safe.

Paige settled next to me, glowing faintly. My skin tingled where our shoulders touched.

"Cassie," she said, "I feel like I should tell you—I'm glad you're the one I can talk to. I'd rather it was you than Mom."

I turned toward her, my throat suddenly tight. "Paige, you don't have to—"

"No, really. I'm not sure why, but I've been thinking about it a lot." She shone brighter, her voice determined. "If it'd been Mom, she wouldn't have known what to do. She'd just have been upset about it. I think it'd have hurt her, seeing me like this, and she wouldn't have wanted to deal with that. But you, like, understand. I can talk to you, and it feels . . . normal."

She threw her arms around and through me so quickly I lost my breath. My bones shivered, in an almost comforting way.

"You're the best sister, Cassie."

"No," I said, grinning, "you are."

We had only been sitting there for a moment when there was a knock on the door. Reluctantly, I got up to answer it.

"Who are you, and what have you done with my daughter?" Dad said, faking shock when I poked my head out. I grimaced at him.

He squeezed my shoulder. "Really, you look wonderful, Cassie."

"And doesn't she!" Mom sidled over, beaming even brighter than Paige had. She winked at me. "My little girl, all grown up."

"Yeah, yeah," I grumbled. If I was going to do this, for real, it was time to get going. My pulse was already racing, urging me to run and hide under the bed until this was all over. I raised my eyebrows at Dad. "You ready?"

He nodded. "I was going to ask you the same thing."

Mom pressed in and hugged me tight. Funny, I'd never noticed how much she smelled like Paige: caramel and spice, except hers was nutmeg to Paige's cinnamon. I relaxed for a second against her, then stepped away.

"All right, let's go."

"As your highness commands." Dad gestured for me to take the stairs first. I ran my fingers over my dress and headed down. The hem rested just high enough on my calves that I didn't have to worry about tripping over it. We'd found it at a little vintage shop: simple, plum-purple polyester. It wasn't quite the gown Mom had been hoping for, but it was one I could live with.

Paige flitted around me as I slid my feet into my new sandals. Being invisible had its benefits: She got to go in her usual halter top and capris, though I bet she'd have traded clothes with me in a second if she could.

We followed Dad out to the car. He opened the passenger door with a flourish.

"Don't be goofy," I told him as I plopped into the seat. "I feel dorky enough as it is."

"Oh?" he said. "I thought it was my duty as a father to make you feel as uncomfortable as possible."

"Well, tonight would be a good time to skip that part of your duty."

"Duly noted."

At the hotel where the prom was being held, it took Dad a while to find a spot to pull over. A bunch of kids had rented limos and took a year getting out of them. Paige leaned over me, peering out the window, gleaming with excitement. The girls clustered together in taffeta and satin while the guys stood by in their identical penguin tuxes and the parents snapped photos. You'd have thought it was the Oscars and not some high school dance.

I couldn't help scanning the heads for that familiar fair hair. Between the distance and the fancy clothes, I couldn't make out anyone I knew at all.

Finally, Dad squeezed in to the curb. "Have a good time," he said. "I'll be here at midnight, but if you want me earlier, just call. Even if it's ten minutes from now."

"I know," I said. "Thanks." I gave him a quick wave and headed up to the front doors. My ticket was jammed into the tiny white purse Mom had lent me; I fumbled for it as my sandals clattered up the steps, making enough noise for three sets of feet. Some of the girls glanced over at me, but all they did was smile. No one was expecting to see Cass McKenna, and no one had ever seen me like this. They didn't know who I was, which was probably for the best. I didn't recognize most of the faces around me either. The golden shine of the hotel lights turned everybody into strangers.

On the third floor, a guy at a banquet table took my ticket and checked his printout. Paige squealed. "That's Kailey Mickelson's brother Bernard," she said. "Wow, he's so much taller than I remember. Kind of cute, too."

"You're at table eighteen," Bernard said to me. "It's to the right, I think." I shot a look at Paige and she floated in with me, grinning madly over her shoulder at him.

Inside the reception room, a couple dozen tables stood under white cloths, set with silverware and lit candles. I sat down carefully, slinging my purse over the back of the chair. Not many people had made it into the room yet. Danielle and Jordana were standing near a raised area with an oak podium at the head of the room, their hands gesturing as fast as their mouths. Funny to think that if a few things had gone differently, back then, I might have been right there with them. Even funnier—thinking that didn't make me feel angry now.

"I wonder what awards they're giving out this year," Paige said, her eyes wide as she took everything in. I cocked an eyebrow at her. "The student council always hands out a bunch of goofy awards, like Cutest Couple and Craziest Comedian. You can guess which one Larry and I got."

My gaze drifted back to the podium, and my heart flipped over. If Tim did make it, that might be the only place I'd see him.

"I'm going to cruise around a bit," Paige said. She giggled and twirled in the air. "This is so much fun! You want to come with?"

I shook my head. If I got back on my feet, I might not be able to stop myself from bolting.

As Paige soared off, bright as a shooting star, I sat there, looking around and trying not to hyperventilate. I started to spot kids from my classes scattered around the tables: the boy in my English class who looked like an eighth-grader, the redheaded girl who chewed gum too loud in math, the guy with the cleft chin who was always leaving geography early for his cross-country meets. Not jerks, not poseurs, just people.

And so far, no sign of Tim. But that didn't mean anything. Maybe he was going for fashionably late.

A couple of girls whisked past me with a gust of citrusy perfume and threw themselves into the chairs on the opposite side of my table. One bent over, giggling, as the other helped her free a lock of hair from the neck of her halter dress. I recognized them, vaguely. Both sophomores, and the girl on the right was on the field hockey team. She glanced at me as her friend straightened up.

"You got stuck at our table?" she said. "That's cool. I'm Meredith."

"Cass."

"Cool," she said again.

The other girl grinned wide enough to show off her multicolored braces. "I'm Ilsa. Are you here by yourself?"

"Um, yeah," I said. "It was kind of a last-minute thing."

"I'm so excited," Meredith said, squirming in her chair. "I've never been to a formal before. I wonder when we get to dance?"

"I don't know."

"We probably eat first, right?" Ilsa said.

I looked quizzically at the menu, which consisted of two main courses, two salads, and two desserts. Pretty short on reading material. I wasn't sure I remembered how to small talk.

The boyfriends saved me. They swooped down on the girls, tossing their suit jackets over the chairs and leaning in close. Senior guys—I could have found their names if I dug in my memory a little. The girls got busy fluttering their eyelashes and forgot about me.

Another couple joined the table just as the waiter arrived. He scribbled down everyone's choices and scurried away, and the newcomers sat down. The girl started chattering away with Meredith and Ilsa, but the guy brushed his lank hair behind his ears and eyed me. I looked down at the table, fiddling with my fork. Keith, I thought. He was on the athletes' committee with Matti and Paul. Oh, God. And now the lynching begins.

"Aren't you—" he started.

"Hey, Keith," one of the other guys interrupted him. "Did your parents let you have the car or what?"

His gaze slid away from me. "Yeah, I finally talked them into it. You'd think I was three years old the way they lectured me. Like I haven't been driving a year and a half already."

I put down my fork and glanced toward the doorway. Any second now, he'd finish that question he'd almost asked.

Paige glided down beside me, glee sparkling from

every pore. "Oh my God, I can't believe how many teachers I still know. I guess they don't change that much. Cass, what's up? You all right?"

I shook my head, slightly. Keith was watching me again.

"Can I do something?" Paige asked. "What's wrong? Maybe—if we go to the washroom, you could tell me there?"

She leaned over my shoulder, inspecting the faces around the table like a cop checking out a lineup. Her hand slipped down and tingled through my shoulder. She hadn't been to a party like this in years, but all it took was a nervous look on my face, and she was there for me, my big sister. I glanced up at her, and the panic in my chest loosened.

I stayed at the edge of my chair, not quite ready to flee, not quite convinced I wouldn't have to. Keith shot a couple more looks my way, and then the conversation absorbed him. In a few minutes, the waiter wobbled over with our salads, and I busied myself with eating. Paige hovered over me, her vigilance fading as she saw me relax. She chattered away about the kids she'd recognized and the dresses she'd liked, and I gave a tiny nod where it seemed necessary. After a while, I even worked up the courage to ask Meredith how the field hockey team was doing. She seemed so overjoyed to have anyone show an interest that she gushed out the details, and I felt bad that I hadn't asked earlier.

I was swirling the last bit of ice cream in the bottom of my dessert bowl when a girl hopped onto the platform and took the podium. I squinted at her against the lights. Dawn, the student council president. My pulse skipped. She flicked her dark hair over her shoulder and smiled against the microphone. "Hey there, Frazer!"

"Hey!" a bunch of kids yelled back.

"As you know," she said, drawling, "tonight's the night we honor our coolest and craziest. We've got all our fantastic prizes. . . ." She swept her arm toward a folding table lined with certificates and gift bags. "Now let's get our cool and crazy council up here!"

Leon and Jordana shimmied between the tables to the platform, where the treasurer and a couple of the senior class reps joined them. I waited, hardly breathing. No one else stood up. Dawn cleared her throat, and the council members took their places to announce the awards.

I sunk down in my chair. So he hadn't come. Well, he was probably still pissed at everyone. He must have assumed I'd been joking, or he was too mad at me to find out. I kicked at the leg of the table. It hardly seemed worth staying now. I'd come, I'd tried it out, I'd shown I could do it. He'd probably never believe me if I told him.

Well, Paige would want to be here for at least a little of the dancing. If I'd survived this long, I could last another half hour.

When the last prize had been handed over and the waiters hurried in to collect the dessert dishes, everyone stood up and flooded out the doors. In the hall, I broke away from the crowd and walked over to the stairs, setting my elbows on the banister and leaning over to watch the people wandering up and down. Paige leaned with me, even though she didn't know who I was looking for. The photography studio had set up a screen on the landing, and the walls rippled with flashes of light.

Inside the reception room, the DJ dimmed the room and put on the music. Red and blue strobe lights flickered. I rubbed my eyes and looked around. Everyone was streaming back into the room, some already bouncing to the music.

Paige leapt toward the doors. "Come on, Cass! This is the best part."

I held back, the shiny dresses and smooth tuxes rippling past me. My chest tightened. This wasn't my scene. You could paint my face from forehead to chin and wrap me in silk, and I still wouldn't belong there.

One song, I thought. I'll stay for one song, let Paige have her fun, and if Tim really hasn't turned up by then, I'll call Dad and get gone.

I dragged myself back into the room. The fringes were packed with kids not quite ready to party. The dance floor whirled with puffy skirts and gyrating limbs, dappled in a rainbow of lights. Paige threw herself in the middle of it, swaying with the melody. All of the tables had been pushed to the side. I crept along the outskirts, feeling my way. The strobe lights flashed, and I thought I saw the glint of Danielle's hair. The faces shone blue, then pink, then green, then back to normal.

By the time the first song blended into the second, there was only a thin ring of us losers still standing to the side of the dance floor. I shifted, staring into the darkness, searching for the chair I'd put my purse on. Maybe on the other side. I scooted around a couple of tables and found it. Swinging it over my shoulder, I turned toward the door, and my eyes stuttered over Tim.

He was standing in the doorway, silhouetted by the lights in the hall behind him, one hand gripping the door frame. I could barely make out his features. He couldn't have seen me at all. I blinked, and he was backing away. His mouth was twisted, his eyes white with panic. The next instant, he vanished from view.

I froze, my heart pounding faster than the music. Had I imagined him?

Before my brain had a chance to consider the question, my legs were already propelling me to the doorway. I peered out, the light dazzling my eyes. Shoes were squeaking on the marble steps below.

"Tim?" I called, hesitantly. A few couples were still hanging out on the landing, getting their pictures taken. Their eyes followed me as I stumbled down the stairs as fast as the sandals would let me. The heels rapped against the marble, even louder than my pulse thumping past my ears. I couldn't hear the squeaking anymore.

Halfway down the last flight, I glanced over the railing and saw him striding across the rug to the hotel's front door. "Tim!" I shouted.

His steps faltered. He turned slowly, as if he wasn't sure he wanted to see who it was. His shoulders were slouched, his hands deep in his pockets, the dress shirt and slacks loose on his gaunt frame. He'd readied his face: mouth tight, eyes defiant. Then he saw me, and it fell apart. His eyebrows drew together in confusion. For a second, he didn't recognize me. But only for a second.

His shoulders stiffened and his jaw went slack. I took advantage of his surprise to stumble down to the bottom of the staircase. The clerk behind the reception desk eyed us blandly, then leaned back in his chair and continued murmuring into the phone.

"Cassie!" Paige yelled from somewhere above. She jumped down to the first floor, stopping a few feet above the ground with a jolt. "Are you going already? You should have told me. I tried to find you, and you weren't there—"

I was still looking at Tim, and he was still looking at me. Paige glanced from me to him and back. "Oh," she said, softly. "Well. Um, I guess I'll wait for you outside." She slipped away through the wall.

"You came," Tim said. His voice was rough. I wanted to believe it wasn't as terse as it had been the last time I'd talked to him, but maybe that was wishful thinking.

"Yeah," I said, feeling awkward in the stupid dress and the stupid sandals and my stupid hairdo—and at the same time, so happy to see him my heart was practically jumping out of my chest. "I'm not sure it was the best idea. But I did say I would—and it wasn't like I could let you be right about me."

The last bit got a twitch out of his lips. Close enough

to a smile that I felt emboldened to add, "I didn't know if you'd make it. After—"

He lowered his eyes. "Yeah, well . . . I figured, hey, if Cass McKenna's going to the prom, I can hardly stay home, right? I guess you did one better than me. I didn't even make it into the room."

"You didn't miss much."

He shrugged, still studying the floor. The silence stretched tight between us. I reached back to grasp the railing of the stairs. "If you were going—I mean, I don't want to bother you."

"Cass," he broke in. He scuffed his feet against the rug. "I've been thinking and talking with my aunt, and I can see why you did it. You really were worried."

"Of course I was worried," I blurted out. "How could you—" I caught myself and curled my fingers into my palms. "I'm still worried. Should I be?"

"I don't think so," he said. "I haven't been drinking. My aunt's helping me find a counselor—she thinks that'll help, too. I've been feeling a lot better, most of the time. It's . . . hard. But not as hard as it used to be."

He looked up at me then, his eyes bright blue under the crystal chandeliers, still carrying so much pain my throat clenched up. "Thank you," he said.

I couldn't quite believe I'd heard him right. "What for?" I asked, cautiously.

"You need me to spell it out?"

I thought of how he'd pushed past me in the parking lot, the skepticism on his face even when tears had been trickling down mine—how I'd stood on his porch while he walked off into his house, his *Go away* echoing in my ears—and swallowed. "Yeah," I said. "I think I do."

"You know, you haven't gotten any easier to talk to," he said, sounding irritated and amused at the same time. "Thank you for trying to help, even though I told you not to."

The tension had been a big balloon, suffocating me from the inside. Those words popped it. I knew I was grinning like a lunatic, but I couldn't seem to stop myself, so I decided not to care.

"You're welcome," I said. "I promise in the future to always try, especially when you're telling me not to."

A smile crept across Tim's face. Not the awkward, pained smile or the horribly desperate smile I'd seen so many times before, but a real smile, soft around the edges. "Deal," he said, and offered his hand so we could shake on it.

"You're going home?" I asked. He glanced past me, up the stairs, and his face tensed again.

"I don't want to see them yet."

"I don't really feel like seeing any more of them either." I nodded toward the front door. "I saw a coffee shop just down the street. You up for an espresso?" When he hesitated, I threw out quickly, "If you just want to leave—"

"No," he said. "I think I can handle a coffee."

We walked outside together, into the glow that spilled out onto the front steps. Paige was perched over the hedge by the sidewalk. She smiled when she saw me, and gave me a thumbs-up with both hands. The sounds of the dance drifted away behind us, and Tim rolled his shoulders. I inhaled deeply, letting the warm air fill my lungs. Tonight was a night when weird things could happen. A night when I could share a table with the student council VP, and my dead sister, too, not to bargain or to prove a point, but simply because I wanted to.

ACKNOWLEDGMENTS

Writers aren't born; they grow. So my first huge thank-you goes to my family, for their love and support; to the teachers who saw a budding author rather than a kid with her head in the clouds, particularly Bert deVries, who always believed there'd be a book with my name on it; and to Chris, for sharing the bouncing-off-the-walls highs and the why-am-I-attempting-this-publishing-thing-again? lows with humor and encouragement.

I owe more than I can express to my fabulous critique partners: Deva Fagan, Amanda Coppedge, and Robin Prehn, who see all the things I miss and said "when" not "if"; the past and present members of the Toronto Speculative Fiction Writers Group, who steer my early drafts straight and deserve gold medals in brainstorming; and Kate Larking, Mary McNeil, Amy Brenham, Amanda Dausman, Sally Holt, and Dorothy Crane, whose thoughtful comments helped shape this novel into what it is today. An additional shout-out to the many writers who shared their experience and enthusiasm throughout this journey, especially the fabulous Debs, who were always there to cheer, advise, and console.

Many, many thanks go to my editor, Robin Tordini, for her careful eye and unflagging devotion to making this book as good as it could be; to Marianne Cohen, Ana Deboo, and April Ward for helping it become a reality; and last but far from least, to my agent, Kristin Nelson, for guiding this book from the slush pile to the bookshelf and never ceasing to amaze me with her dedication and drive.